10/19

Etty Steele
Vampire Hunter

GRAYSON GRAVE

CHAPTER 1

I WAS SITTING at the kitchen table eating cereal with extra milk so that the chocolatey loops floated around. I imagined they were sailors lost at sea. One by one I saved them with my spoon from the milky waters.

It was the first day of school after the summer holidays and I wasn't used to getting up this early. I had sleepy eyes and I kept laying my forehead against the table, hoping I could fall asleep again without Mum noticing.

"Wake up!" she snapped from the sink, where she was washing up. She flicked water at me and I groaned as it hit me in the face. Drops slid down to my chin.

"You got it in my breakfast," I said. There were washing-up bubbles in my cereal.

That was when Dad walked in. He looked even sleepier than I felt. There were purple bags under his eyes and his hair stuck up in all directions. He smiled at Mum and hugged her. After that, he held out his hands and Mum happily took off the rubber gloves and handed them to him. Dad always did the housework.

He turned to me and gave me a kiss on the forehead.

"Morning, sweetheart," he said. But, a moment later, Mum had come between us. She snatched my bowl and shoved it into Dad's hands.

"Wash that up, darling," she said to him. "As for you, Henrietta, you're coming with me to the training room. Now!"

She grabbed my hand and marched me into the hallway.

"For the hundredth time," I said, "please don't call me Henrietta."

Mum opened the secret panel in the wall and revealed the hidden keypad with the numbers 0–9 on it. She quickly typed in the code (which she kept a secret from Dad and me) and then slid the panel closed again. The door to the basement popped open.

"Henrietta is your name," Mum said, shaking her head. She was looking at me like I wasn't really her daughter but an alien who'd been sent down from space.

"I hate Henrietta," I told her as we walked down the stairs to the basement. "You know I hate it. Everyone else calls me Etty. You're the only one who still calls me that awful name."

We reached the bottom of the stairs, where it was so dark that I couldn't see. I reached for the light switch.

"Henrietta was your great-grandmother's name," Mum said irritably. "Now it's your name, and I'm not going to call you anything else."

I rolled my eyes and then my fingers found the light switch, which made the room buzz with electricity when I turned it on.

The basement underneath my house wasn't a normal

kind of basement. In fact, you might think you'd time-travelled to the future if you saw it – or you might think my family were slightly insane. The walls and ceiling were made of metal and the floor was black and shiny – it looked like black glass. That wasn't the strangest bit, though. There was a punch bag; lots of human dummies; a set of weapons attached to the wall; a robot that looked like a faceless, plastic human; a white circle painted on the floor and two wooden battle sticks hanging from the ceiling on clips. There were also wooden chests and cabinets against the walls. I'd never been allowed to open these. They were always locked.

Our house definitely wasn't normal, especially not for the town we lived in. Brightwood was a small town near the sea, full of fishermen and farmers. Basements like this weren't supposed to exist in such a quiet, old-fashioned place.

As I walked into the circle on the floor, Mum unclipped the battle sticks and threw one to me. I'd only just caught it when she came charging towards me, her stick raised above her head.

CHAPTER 2

I BLOCKED MUM'S attack with my stick and then spun behind her and aimed a strike at her shoulder. She was quick. She ducked and rolled across the floor, springing back to her feet. My mum was agile, like a cat. But so was I. We carried on sparring, dodging around one another. Soon, I was sweating and my hands were sore from gripping the stick. Mum wasn't even tired. She ducked and leapt and spun around me while I struggled not to let her touch me with her stick. If she did, it meant I lost.

For once – just once – I wanted to win.

Then I saw my chance. Mum had jumped out of the way of my last attack and she'd stumbled and fallen. I was about to catch her arm with my stick when I heard her gasp in pain. Had she hurt herself? Maybe she'd twisted her ankle. I stopped before my stick touched her, and held out my hand to see if she was all right.

"Tricked you!" she said, grabbing my arm with one hand and pressing her stick against my chest with the other.

I blinked in shock.

She'd won.

She straightened her leg and smiled in triumph. She was absolutely fine. She'd been faking it.

"That's not fair!" I said, my hands trembling.

"You shouldn't have stopped," she replied matter-of-factly. "You're too soft, Henrietta. You must never stop – never give your enemy a chance to get the upper hand."

"I thought you were really hurt," I said, throwing the stick on the floor angrily and folding my arms across my chest.

"Pick that up and stop acting so spoilt," she barked.

I could feel my face going pale. I quickly did as she asked. When I placed the stick in her hand, she laid it against my shoulder.

"I expect more of you, Henrietta," she said. "This isn't a game. If I don't teach you right, you could get hurt."

"I would have won if you hadn't cheated," I told her.

"Then be smarter and beat me next time."

"That's what I've been trying to do," I said. I turned and headed towards the staircase.

"Try harder!" she called after me in a stern voice. "You're a vampire hunter, and it's time you started acting like one."

I narrowed my eyes and then stormed off to get ready for school.

CHAPTER 3

YOU PROBABLY THOUGHT vampires weren't real, right? Well, they are. Mum worked for a company that paid her to catch them. Dad, on the other hand, worked in a supermarket and had to wear a neon t-shirt with a name badge pinned on it.

You see, my mum's family has hunted vampires for generations. I was the next in a long line of hunters. Our job was to keep people safe. Vampires were dangerous and emotionless. They were strong and fast, and they drank human blood. It was up to hunters to track them down, capture them, and send them to Traxis – a secret island north of Scotland. If a vampire was sent to Traxis, they never came back. Thankfully, hunters had special abilities too. We were strong and fast like vampires. Well, most hunters were...

I, on the other hand, was not super-fast, super-strong – or super-anything for that matter.

"Your powers will come," Mum used to tell me. Now, however, she avoided the subject. I shuddered at the thought of our trip into the mountains. Mum had taken me camping over the summer to try to speed up my slow progress. She said that was how she'd discovered her hunter powers when she was my age. We went on long hikes that blistered my feet, battled with wooden swords that left my wrists aching, and camped in the wild in a tent that was only just large enough for the two of us.

One night, she took me to a mountain cave to look for bats. It was pitch-black and she said we couldn't use torches. I shivered at the thought of bats watching us from the shadows. I kept my eyes alert: old vampires had the power to turn into bats.

"Do you sense any vampires?" I asked.

"No," she said. "It's too cold and uncomfortable."

"Then why are we here?"

"Training," she answered as if it had been obvious.

After what felt like hours of searching, we found their roost. The bats hardly moved. We sat there watching them for the rest of the night. Most of them hung upside-down from the roof of the cave, as still as stone.

Mum told me I needed to be able to spot a bat from far away, hear them and know how to hide from them. If a vampire transformed into a bat, they could easily escape capture. I had to be able to track them in human form and in bat form.

We went back to the cave night after night.

"How does a vampire learn to become a bat?" I asked one evening as we leaned against the cave wall, watching the roost. My back was sore and my toes were numb. I hoped that talking would distract me.

"Henrietta, vampires are pure evil and they drink human blood. That's all you need to know."

"There's got to be more to them," I said.

"Humans get bitten," Mum said irritably, "then they turn into vampires. They get stronger every year, and after a few hundred years they gain other powers as well. That's it."

I already know all that, I thought. But, before I could ask anything else, she pulled a strange-looking weapon from her belt. It was a short metal knife, the length of a teaspoon, with a wooden point at one end.

I recognised the wood from my training. It was red oak. Since wood was the only thing that could hurt vampires, I'd learned all the different types years ago.

Mum twirled the strange little weapon in her fingers. "Do you know what this is?" she asked.

I shrugged.

"It's a throwing stake," she told me. "A vampire once tried to escape from me. He thought it would be safe, flying off in bat form. The fool. I hit him in the wing with one of these." She held up the throwing stake, stroking its polished, red oak point. "The metal makes it heavy, so it flies better. The oak makes it lethal. The vampire was easy to trap once I took him down."

Without a flicker of hesitation, she took aim and threw the weapon straight into the heart of the bats' roost. One of the bats dropped to the floor like dead fruit from a tree. The cave exploded with dark, flapping shapes. My heart skipped a beat as they screeched and squealed.

"That's how you kill a vampire," Mum whispered triumphantly.

It wasn't a vampire, though, I'd thought, staring at the dead animal and then at Mum's weapon sticking out of its little chest. *It was just a bat.*

After three weeks in the mountains, I had not changed. I was no stronger or faster than before.

Ever since we'd returned, Mum had been giving me these sad, disappointed looks whenever we trained. I had never beaten her in battle. Not once. I felt useless, ashamed.

What if my superpowers *never* came?

As I got ready for school, I thought about the way she'd tricked me so she could win our training battle. She'd said I was wrong to check if she was okay. If a vampire had tricked me like that, I could've been killed…

Vampires heal within minutes. That's what Mum had always told me. *Only a wooden stake will really hurt them.*

So was she right? Was I being too soft?

I frowned. Hurting someone who was already injured just felt wrong, even if they were a vampire.

I put on my grey trousers and white blouse and picked up my blue jumper, which had the school logo on it. Sunlight shone through my window. It was going to be a hot day. April would probably wear her blue and white summer dress to school. A smile spread across my face at the thought of seeing my friend. Her full name was April Showers. April Showers. She was probably the only person I knew who hated her name more than I hated mine.

My stomach clenched uncomfortably when I remembered the last time we'd spoken on the phone. She'd tried to meet up with me over the summer, but I'd been away camping in the mountains. When we got back, Mum had told me I wasn't allowed to go anywhere or see anyone.

"Training comes first, Henrietta," she'd said.

So, in six whole weeks, I hadn't seen April at all.

As I finished getting ready for school, I couldn't help

doing a few press-ups and then some high-speed running on the spot. Afterwards, I stood in front of the mirror. April would definitely wear a summer dress, but I was much happier in my school trousers and white shirt. I wasn't a dress kind of girl.

I flexed my arms. Although I had muscles, they weren't very impressive. I sighed and pulled my brown hair back into a ponytail – like always. A long time ago, Dad had put ribbons in my hair and people had called me pretty. But, when Mum had caught me staring at them in the mirror, she'd tugged at one of the ribbons and then sent me a look. I'd known what it had meant – *Hunters don't wear pretty ribbons in their hair.* A few days later, I'd burned them and sprinkled the ashes in the bin.

"Etty!" Dad called from downstairs, distracting me from my memories. "Time to go, sweetie!"

Those words sent butterflies flapping in my stomach. Soon, I'd be back at school. I'd be in Year 6 with a new teacher – Miss Gravel. The only good part of it was that I'd get to see April again. I only hoped she wouldn't be too upset with me for being such a lousy friend.

After grabbing my bag, I headed downstairs to find Dad waiting. He handed me my lunchbox and we left the house. Taking a deep breath, I stepped outside.

Dad's truck was an old thing that had peeling red paint and whined going uphill. We were quiet as he drove along the country lanes. We had to pass three farms and then cross Barley Bridge before we got to the town. Because Dad used to be a fisherman, our house was way out of town, close to the harbour.

People waved at Dad as we drove past them. Brightwood

was a small town, and Dad was one of those people who got on with everyone he met. It was a real problem if you were trying to get somewhere in a hurry – farmers, nosy residents, shop owners or just random people in the street would regularly stop to chat to him.

Now, as we drove through the centre of town, I watched the people in the market setting up their stalls. Half of them shouted 'good morning' to Dad as we passed. At the weekend, the town square would be full of tourists buying fridge magnets, ice creams and buckets and spades for the beach. Not to mention the fake 'witchy things' like crystal balls and plastic cauldrons that were always on sale. The shop and stall-owners supported the myth that witches used to live in Brightwood hundreds of years ago. The stone circle on Mulberry Hill was said to have been used by witches in the olden days. Of course, no one believed witches ever existed, but it meant tourists would buy fake witch's fingers and tacky broomsticks.

I glanced down Sage Lane as we passed it. In the distance, I could see Baywater Beach – the main beach in Brightwood. More tourist shops lined the street. I smiled as I thought of April complaining about the lack of 'real shops' in Brightwood.

It's impossible to buy clothes, she'd say.

Thankfully, I hated shopping so it didn't bother me.

As school came into sight, I shrank in my seat. The million-year-old building looked like a haunted house and it contained the evillest thing in the world – schoolwork.

Here we go again, I thought.

CHAPTER 4

"ARE YOU OKAY?" Dad asked, pulling up outside school. The truck windows were down but it was still boiling. The sunlight shone fiercely through the windscreen.

"I'm fine," I replied. "Just a bit nervous."

"You haven't seen your friends in a while," he said, looking at me with worry.

"I only have one friend, Dad," I reminded him. "I just hope she's not too mad at me."

"Then invite April over," he said. "Tell her she can come around after school."

I stared at him for a long moment, shocked. "Dad? Are you feeling okay? You know Mum will go insane if I bring April home."

"I know, but—"

"What if I miss training?" I interrupted.

"Invite her over," Dad said, his voice uncharacteristically firm. "I'll cook my famous lasagne. And don't worry about your mother. I'll speak to her."

I wasn't sure how to react. What would Mum say?

Surely it won't hurt to miss one day of training, I thought.

I saw April in the cloakroom, hanging up her bag. Her nails were painted yellow. I never painted my nails. If I did, I would paint them black. She'd also had her hair cut. It had hung down to her waist before, but now it was just below her shoulders. Its colour hadn't changed, though – bright blonde. Her stud earrings were silver stars.

"Hey," I said awkwardly, coming to stand next to her.

April tucked her hair behind her ears and smiled. "Etty," she said shyly in her quiet voice.

"I knew it," I said.

"What?" she asked.

"You always wear a summer dress when it's hot."

She laughed. "And you wear trousers, even when it's one hundred degrees."

"True," I agreed, grinning.

We headed into class and sat down next to each other at the back. When April opened her pencil case to take out her pen, I noticed she wore a ring. It had a gold band with a yellow, triangle-shaped gem set into the metal. The colour of the gem matched the wheat-yellow of her hair.

"Where'd you get that?" I asked.

She quickly covered the ring with her other hand. Her cheeks went pink. "It's nothing," she said.

"It looks expensive."

"It isn't." She pulled her hands under the desk so the ring was hidden from sight.

That was weird.

Before I could say any more about it, she asked me if I'd had a good summer. I told her I'd spent it helping my mum train for another kickboxing championship (that was my cover story for vampire hunter training). When I asked April about her holiday, she shrugged.

"I didn't really do a lot," she said. "I practised my violin and I helped Grandma out with some stuff..." Her voice trailed off.

My heart sank. Her summer had been rubbish. "Is your grandma still as crazy as ever?" I asked, trying to make her smile.

"Crazier," April replied, her tone serious. "She's started sprinkling herbs across the windowsills and doorways to ward off 'dark energy'. Ever since her friend – you know..."

"I know," I said. Her grandma's friend, Helen – an old woman who had lived alone in a house by the beach – had died unexpectedly a few weeks ago. No one knew exactly how Helen had died.

"I'm worried about Grandma," April said. "She's always been a bit odd, but she's been saying some really weird things lately."

"Like what?"

"Just... stuff," she said, her eyebrows drawing together.

We were silent for a while. I tried to think of something to say.

"I lied," she said suddenly. "My summer wasn't okay. It was terrible. I got so bored that I even started helping Grandma weed the garden."

"I'm sorry," I told her, feeling guilty. "I should've been around. But I can make it up to you. Dad gave me permission to invite you over after school – if you want."

April's mouth fell open. "To your house?" she asked. "I've never seen inside your house before."

"Dad thought it would be a good idea."

"And what about your mum?" she asked warily.

I decided to avoid that question. "Can you come?"

She grinned and nodded enthusiastically.

Then Miss Gravel stepped forward to introduce herself. She was young for a teacher, with red hair and kind eyes that were half hidden behind a pair of stylish glasses. Halfway through taking the register, she called out, "Vladimir Nox."

The class looked at her in confusion. Vladimir Nox? Who was that?

No one answered.

"Vladimir?" she called again. After a moment, she moved on.

At the end of the register, Miss Gravel stood up and told us there would be a new boy joining the class. "Unfortunately," she said, "he doesn't seem to be in school yet. Now, I want you all to be kind and welcoming to him when he arrives. You all know how scary it is starting a new school."

For the rest of the day, we were on the lookout for the new boy, but he didn't show up. By the end of the day, the class was buzzing with theories about Vladimir Nox. Some of the girls thought he sounded exotic. One girl declared that she was in love with him already.

"I hope he's nice," April said as we got our home things from our pegs. "We could add another friend to our group."

"We'd be the weirdest named group in the world," I replied. "Henrietta Steele, April Showers and Vladimir Nox."

April burst into laughter.

Once we were outside, we ran over to April's grandma's rickety car, a blue VW Beetle that looked like it was about to fall apart. April's grandma (who everyone called Grandma Elsie) looked young for such an old person. She wore headscarves in varying shades of blue and lots of necklaces with crystals hanging from them. One particular necklace had always fascinated me, with its gold chain and the three hourglasses attached to it. Elsie's earrings were always long and dangly, and her hair, which I think should have been grey, was dyed blonde.

She already had her window down when we reached the car and she was humming along to an old song that I didn't recognise. Before April could open her mouth to speak, Grandma Elsie said, "Of course you can spend the evening at Etty's. I'll pick you up at eight."

April and I exchanged a look. Her grandma had a habit of doing that – somehow knowing what you were going to say before you said it. It was one of the many things that made her seem so odd.

Inside her car, I noticed there was a line of green herbs spread across the dashboard.

"Um, thanks," April replied.

She waved goodbye to her grandma and followed me to my dad's truck.

Once we'd climbed inside and fastened our seatbelts, Dad revved the engine and we sped off.

As we drove home, I couldn't stop smiling.

CHAPTER 5

MUM WASN'T HOME. I sighed in relief. April took off her shoes and stood awkwardly in the hallway while Dad offered us a choice of drinks: iced tea, cola, lemonade, orangeade… The list went on and on. I never usually had so many options. April chose iced tea. I could hear Mum's voice yelling in my head about 'evil sugar' so I chose water.

As soon as we'd finished our drinks, I whisked April upstairs. I was about to open the door to my room when I had a sudden panic. Had I left it in a mess? I tried to remember.

I hope there's no dirty washing on the floor, I thought.

Trying to stay calm, I opened the door and led April inside. She looked around at the grey walls and black furniture, then down at the floorboards, which were also painted grey.

"Wow," she said.

"What?" I asked, scanning the room for anything embarrassing. Thankfully, everything was tidy.

"You really don't like colour, do you?" she said. "I've never seen so much grey."

She walked over to the window and gazed out at the street. My heart leapt into my throat. Next to her, on top of the chest of drawers, was my hunting stake (an ironwood stake I'd carved and sharpened myself). The length of a pencil, it was as thick as a broomstick and had an ultra-sharp point at one end. It was a weapon for fighting vampires and definitely not something a ten-year-old was meant to have in their room.

What was I going to do?

While she wasn't looking, I crept over to the stake and picked it up – but before I could put it away, she turned around. Quickly, I hid the weapon behind my back.

"You've never liked girly things," she said. "You must think my room is a nightmare."

"Well, your room does sort of look like a unicorn's vomited everywhere," I replied jokingly.

She giggled.

I held tightly to the stake. "Seriously, though, your room suits you. It's bright and cheerful – just like you. And it's full of books – you know, because you're a nerd."

She flicked me in the chest. "There's nothing wrong with being a nerd," she said defensively, "and books are great. Crime thrillers and murder mysteries are the best."

I gestured around at my room. "Well, as you can see, there are no books in this room." I'd said it in a humorous voice, but my face flushed. I didn't want to talk about my difficulty reading, my low reading scores, especially not that I was given extra help in lessons. These things had never bothered me much when I was younger, but now it felt embarrassing. Mum didn't understand the problem. Apparently, reading wasn't as important as learning to fight or being able to whittle a stake. Maybe she was right, but her opinion hadn't done me any favours at school.

"Can I sit down?" April asked, changing the subject.

"Of course," I replied. Keeping my hands behind my back, I sat beside her on the bed. Sneakily, I slid the stake under the covers. My heart rate started to slow down. *That was close.*

"Do you remember when we were in Year 1?" she asked. "You kept fighting with the boys in class and getting sent to the head teacher."

I'd forgotten about that. The teachers thought I was a menace. They had to call in my parents.

"And then in Year 2," April said, "one of the boys stole your pencil. You went so red and you were shaking. I knew you were going to attack him and I didn't want you to get in trouble. Do you remember?"

"You gave me your pencil instead," I replied, "and I calmed down."

"That's when we became friends," she said.

"No, it was before that," I told her. "Lucy wouldn't let you be the princess in the dressing-up area, so I ripped the dress off her and gave it to you."

"I forgot about that!" April said, laughing. "The dress was so ripped, I couldn't wear it. I cried because it was ruined."

I laughed with her and we tried to remember other funny stories. We talked about our memories until Dad called us down for dinner.

Mum was there. She greeted April with a tight smile. She didn't say much during dinner but Dad was chatty, so it wasn't too awkward.

When it was time for her to leave, April picked up her

bag from the hall and slipped on her shoes. As she tied her laces, her ring glinted in the light from the open door. The sun was setting and it bathed the hallway in an orange glow. My parents were in the kitchen, talking in sharp but quiet voices. They were arguing. April pretended she couldn't hear them.

"Are you going to tell me about the ring?" I asked her.

It took her a while to reply. "Grandma gave it to me," she said finally.

I could tell there was more to it. "April, what is it?"

"It's just... You know when I said Grandma has been acting stranger than usual? Well, she thinks..."

"What?" I pressed.

"When I was little, she used to tell me stories about fairies and witches and vampires, except she always said they weren't just stories. She thought they were true, that magic was real."

My eyes widened.

"I know, it's insane," April said. "But recently, she's been saying her friend Helen's death wasn't natural. She thinks it was to do with magic. She told me she's a witch – and I'm a witch too."

"You're a witch?" I asked sceptically. I knew vampires existed, but I'd never heard Mum mention witches before. It was just an old folk tale that witches once lived in Brightwood. No one actually thought it was true.

April lifted her hand to show me the ring. "Grandma made me wear this. She says I'm nearly eleven so I'll be getting my 'powers' soon. The ring is meant to help me understand them. She made me try on about ten different rings until she decided this one was right."

I couldn't help it. My lips curved into a smile.

"It's not funny," April said, whacking me lightly on the arm.

Then April's grandma pulled up outside the house in her dilapidated car.

"You think Gran's mad," April said.

"Only a little," I replied, trying to fight the smile.

She sighed before saying a quick goodbye and then jogging across the front lawn.

"Don't cast any spells!" I called out.

She poked her tongue out at me and got in the car. When April's grandma drove off, the engine growled like it was in pain. Behind me, my parents continued to argue, and so I slipped upstairs to my room.

CHAPTER 6

THE NEXT DAY, I was late for school. I hadn't slept very well. Mum and Dad had spent most of the night arguing – and I knew it was because I'd invited April over. Mum made me get up early to do extra training and I bruised my arm falling over during our stick battle.

"Get up," she'd ordered. "Vampires heal quickly. They won't give you a rest. You need to ignore the pain and keep fighting."

I'd sprung to my feet and attacked her with my battle stick.

At the end of our fight, she'd thrown me a towel and crossed her arms. "A thirty-year-old vampire might have trouble against you," she said. "They are young and their strength hasn't come yet, but a vampire in their hundreds: you'd be dead in less than a minute."

"I don't have my powers yet," I said. "I'm not a full hunter."

"I know," she replied quietly. "That's what I'm worried about."

When I walked into class, everyone else was already sitting down. Miss Gravel smiled as I made my way over to my seat.

"Are you all right?" April asked in a whisper. "You look like you haven't slept."

I opened my mouth to reply but I didn't know what to say. I couldn't tell her the truth.

She started fiddling nervously with the yellow ring on her finger. "I need to talk to you," she said. "I'm worried about—"

But before she could finish her sentence, Miss Gravel cleared her throat.

"Good morning, class," she said. "As you know, we have a new boy starting today." She gestured towards a student sitting in the front row. I hadn't noticed him before. He stood up and Miss Gravel led him to the front of the class.

The moment he turned around, my heart skipped a beat.

His hair was black, his skin was pale, his lips were red – and, when he smiled, his teeth were pure white. What really caught my eye, however, were his black sunglasses.

My hands gripped the desk.

"This is Vladimir Nox," Miss Gravel said.

Is he…? I thought in panic. *No. No. He can't be.*

He was wearing a cardigan (black, without a school logo on it) even though it was a hot day. He had a white shirt on with a purple bowtie. His outfit was old-fashioned, like he'd been dressed by a grandma – or by someone very old…

Vampires lived for hundreds of years.

Fearfully, I tried to remember everything Mum had told me about how to spot a vampire:

1. Eyes. Vampires always had really big pupils. That meant they couldn't see very well in bright light.

   He's wearing sunglasses! Indoors!

2. Teeth. Vampires' teeth never got stained or damaged, so they were usually extremely white and perfectly even.

   Okay, so he has sunglasses on and perfectly white teeth. That doesn't mean he's a vampire!

3. Skin. The skin of a vampire was always pale because the sun was painful to them. Their skin was also colder than a human's.

   Well, he's definitely pale. But maybe he plays video games in his room all day and doesn't go out much.

4. Smell. Most vampires smelled strongly of either garlic, cabbage, sewage or blood.

   I can't smell him from here.

I was going to have to get closer. I also needed to check his nails. Vampires' nails didn't have white tips at the end, like human nails.

"He seems nice," April whispered in my ear. "It takes a lot of courage to wear a bowtie on the first day of school. Especially a purple one."

Around the classroom, I could see other people whispering and giggling. I guessed the vampire boy did look a bit odd with that purple bowtie. I just hoped he wouldn't see people laughing and take his revenge by drinking everyone's blood!

"Does anyone have a question for Vladimir?" Miss Gravel asked the class.

Sophie Edwards put her hand up. "Why are you wearing sunglasses?" she asked with a nasty smirk.

Vladimir's voice was quiet and nervous. "I-I'm sensitive to the light," he said.

"You look weird!" shouted Lori Pullman.

Vladimir's pale cheeks turned pink.

He's going to get angry and kill us all! I thought.

Miss Gravel sent him back to his seat and started the lesson, but I couldn't concentrate. My eyes were fixed on the back of Vladimir's head.

A vampire, I thought. *There's a vampire in my class!*

CHAPTER 7

AT BREAK, I tried to follow Vladimir out of class but April pulled me to one side in the cloakroom and held up her right hand. The yellow ring gleamed. Behind her, Vladimir disappeared into the crowd.

"What's wrong?" I asked.

She bit her lip. "I can't take it off."

"What do you mean?"

"The ring," she said. "It won't come off. Grandma says that proves I'm a witch."

Clasping the ring between my fingers, I tugged. It didn't budge. When I pulled harder, heat seared my fingers. I winced and jerked my hand away. I saw, to my shock, that my skin was burned. It stung, and I gritted my teeth.

"What?" she asked. "What is it?"

I closed my fist to hide my fingers. "Nothing," I lied, trying to keep my face calm.

It just burned me! I thought. *The ring just burned me!*

Did that mean magic was real? Was April a witch?

"Something's wrong," she said. "Tell me."

She looked worried enough. She didn't need to know the ring could burn people too. "It's just stuck, that's all," I told her calmly.

"What if it never comes off?" she asked.

"April," I said, "it's only a ring."

She nodded, unconvinced. I kept my hand clenched in a fist. There had to be an explanation. Maybe I'd just got an electric shock. When April wasn't paying attention, I checked my fingers. There was a thin line of pink across the skin.

Weird, I thought as we walked out to the playground together. Could it be possible that witches were real? After all, vampires existed, and they were supposed to be a myth. Did that mean werewolves and demons were more than just fairy stories as well? The thought made me uneasy.

As we made our way to the benches on the playground, I kept my eyes peeled for any sign of Vladimir. April might be a witch, but my biggest priority was the fact that there was a vampire in my class. I had to focus on Vladimir. After all, he could be out there sucking someone's blood right this minute.

I was vaguely aware of April talking to me and I tried to follow along to what she said, but I couldn't help tuning in and out.

"Etty, are you listening to me?" she asked after a while.

"Sorry?"

"Never mind," she said. The note of disappointment in her voice made me wince. After that, we didn't say much. April went to chat with some of her other friends, leaving me alone on the bench. I sighed as I scanned the crowd for Vladimir. But by the end of break I still hadn't spotted him.

I vowed that at lunch I wouldn't let him get away.

The rest of the morning's lessons seemed to go on

forever. I didn't pay attention to anything Miss Gravel said (which wasn't hard since it was English and we were reading a book I could barely follow). Instead, I spent most of the time staring at the back of Vladimir's head.

Finally, the bell rang for lunch. I hurried out of class, following Vladimir. He wasn't going to escape again.

He took his lunchbox and hurried down the corridor… in the wrong direction. The lunch hall was the other way. Quickly, I grabbed my lunch and, behind me, April did the same.

"Where are we going?" she asked as she followed me along the corridor.

Gently, I shushed her. "He'll hear you."

"Who?"

I didn't answer because, at that moment, Vladimir disappeared through a door further along the corridor.

"Follow me," I told her.

I approached the door slowly and then peered through the little window. It was an empty classroom.

Sitting on his own at one of the desks was Vladimir. He had his lunchbox in front of him. There was no one else in there.

Not sure what I was going to do, I opened the door and walked inside. Vladimir quickly shut the lid of his lunchbox (which was purple and glittery). I wondered what was inside it. Vampires didn't eat. They drank blood. So what could he be eating for lunch?

"H-hello," he said softly.

April entered the room before I could stop her, her lunchbox at her side. She tucked her hair behind her ear and smiled shyly.

"I'm April," she said. "You're Vladimir?"

My nerves were shredded. I was afraid that, at any moment, Vladimir would grip her by the shoulders and sink his teeth into her neck. Why had I brought her with me? How could I have been so stupid?

Vladimir's cheeks turned pink. "H-hi," he said. "Please call me Dimi. I hate Vladimir."

I stepped forward, ready to protect April if I needed to. "Why are you hiding in here?" I asked him suspiciously.

"I'm n-not hiding," he replied. "I just d-d-don't know anyone yet."

"Dimi," April said, "you're not going to make any friends sitting in here on your own."

His shoulders slumped. "I-I'm fine."

"You can't eat by yourself on your first day," she said. "We'll eat in here with you."

I tried not to show my panic. We couldn't stay in here with him! What if he decided to eat *us* instead of his lunch? "No," I said. "We should take Dimi to the lunch hall."

"But he's nervous," April replied.

I frowned at her but I knew from the look on her face that she wasn't going to change her mind. "Fine," I said.

We all sat down and started eating. I watched carefully as Dimi opened his lunchbox. Inside, I saw nothing unusual. There were carrot sticks, sandwiches, and cheese and onion crisps.

"So," April said, "have you just moved to Brightwood?"

"N-no," Dimi replied. "I've always lived here with my dad."

"I've never seen you around," April commented.

Dimi picked up a carrot stick and fiddled with it. "My d-dad's a bit protective. I-I don't get out much."

"You don't like the sun?" I asked in a sharp voice.

"N-no, it's not that," Dimi replied. "My mum d-died when I was young. Dad is worried that… I think he w-wants to keep me safe."

"Oh," April said and she leaned forward an inch. There was a definite spark of interest in her eyes. Was she thinking of her own parents? She'd never really spoken about them other than to tell me they'd died when she was young. The thought of her sharing her painful memories with a vampire-in-disguise made me grit my teeth.

I folded my arms. "So why are you here if your dad wants to keep you safe at home?" Was it to suck all of our blood? Were you hoping schoolkids would be easy prey?

"I-I used to be home-schooled," he replied. "But our house was broken into w-when I was home with Maggie – my tutor. I didn't see who the intruders were. Maggie took me to the s-safe room as soon as we heard them break the door down. But now Dad thinks I-I'll be safer at school." The way he said it, it sounded like he didn't agree. Maybe he didn't want to be here after all. Perhaps he was on some kind of vampire mission he couldn't get out of.

I narrowed my eyes.

I leaned forward, wishing I could see through his sunglasses – it might have helped me figure out if he was lying.

I had the feeling there was something he wasn't telling us. If Dimi was a vampire, how could he have a dad? His real, human dad couldn't possibly be looking after him – Dimi would have drunk his blood by now. Unless his dad had been bitten too? Maybe they'd both been turned into vampires at the same time…

There was also the strange fact that Dimi's house had been

broken into. Had his Dad really sent Dimi to school because he was worried about his safety? Since when did vampires fear robbers? There had to be another reason Dimi was at school, and I was sure it wasn't to be safe from petty criminals.

April was wide-eyed. "That must've been petrifying," she said. "Lucky you have a safe room…"

"It wasn't too bad," he said. "Not lucky, really. D-Dad's safety mad."

April reached out to take his hand. Awkwardly, he lifted the carrot stick to his mouth, avoiding her touch. "Um, what was it like being home-schooled?" April asked, returning her hand to rest on her polka dot lunchbox.

"It was great," Dimi said. "Maggie looked after me while Dad was at work. She taught me all the usual subjects. But m-my favourite lesson was dance. She u-used to be a ballet teacher. She was the one who said I had to dress smart for my first day…"

"Well, you are dressed smart," April remarked, smiling encouragingly. "I like your bowtie."

"Thanks," he replied. "N-no one else is wearing one, though. I think Maggie was a bit old-fashioned. She was eighty."

Looking uncomfortable, Dimi lifted his drink out of his lunchbox.

I gasped.

His bottle was filled with red liquid. Red! Not only that but, as he picked it up, I noticed his nails were see-through – they had no white part!

"What's that?" April asked, inspecting his drink.

"Oh…" Dimi replied. He paused and I watched him closely, wondering what he would say. "It's cranberry juice."

Cranberry juice? I thought. *Blood, you mean.*

"Oh," April replied. "I've never had that. Can I try some?"

I almost choked on my apple.

"Sure," Dimi said, passing the bottle to her.

She couldn't drink it! It was blood! It had to be blood!

April took the bottle. She lifted it up to her mouth.

"No!" I shouted and shot out my hand. Time seemed to slow down as two things happened at once:

1. The bottle flew out of April's hand and landed on the floor.
2. I accidentally elbowed Dimi in the face, which made his sunglasses slip off.

Quickly, he put them back on but for a split second I caught sight of Dimi's pupils. They were huge – just like a vampire's.

My blood turned cold. *He is a vampire!* I thought. *He must be!*

April and Dimi watched the red puddle of his drink spread across the floor.

"Etty!" April said.

Dimi was still staring at his spilled drink.

I picked up my lunchbox and took April by the arm. "Come on!" I said. "We're leaving!"

"What?"

She grabbed her lunchbox as I dragged her out of the room, leaving Dimi alone behind us.

There was no doubt about it.

He was a vampire.

And I wasn't supposed to sit and make friends with vampires. I was supposed to hunt them.

CHAPTER 8

APRIL WOULDN'T TALK to me for the rest of lunch.

When we got back to class, Dimi walked in with tear tracks down his face and blotchy, red cheeks. He carried his lunchbox. Miss Gravel reminded him to put it back on the trolley –and then people started noticing that it was purple and glittery. Whispers and giggles spread through the classroom.

Dimi backed away. He looked like he was about to start crying. For a moment, I felt sorry for him.

He's a vampire! I reminded myself. *He drinks human blood! He's evil!*

April still wouldn't talk to me as we waited to be picked up at the end of the day, and I was glad when Dad arrived to take me home. He asked me how my day had been and, after I mumbled something in reply, we were silent. My mind was too busy for me to talk.

I didn't say much at dinner either. I couldn't stop think-ing about Dimi – and wondering if I should tell Mum about him.

Not yet, I thought. *I don't have enough proof. I don't want to get it wrong again! Not like last time...*

That's right. I was wary because this had happened before.

In Year 3, I had been sure that the new boy in our class, Bane Larkin, was a vampire. He'd had all the signs:

1. Black hair.
2. Pale skin.
3. White teeth.
4. Nails bitten down so the whites couldn't be seen.

Oh, and he was also pure evil!

In Bane's first week, he'd found out that April was afraid of worms so, when he saw a big, fat one on the field a few days later, he'd taken it and hidden it in her lunchbox. She'd screamed when she saw it wriggling in her sandwich. Horrified, she'd tried to run away but she hadn't realised that Bane Larkin was standing behind her. He'd smirked – and then pulled out another worm and dropped it in her hair!

I went crazy. I charged at him like a rhino but some older kids grabbed me and held me down until a teacher came along. Like a crazy animal, I bit and scratched them. He'd put a worm in April's hair! I wanted to murder him!

April had cried for the rest of the day and had to be taken home. I'd been sent to the head teacher's office to calm down.

That evening, I'd told Mum all about Bane. She'd said we would have to test him to check if he really was a vampire.

"It's rare," she'd said, "for someone so young to be turned into a vampire."

When I'd asked her why, she told me it was unnatural.

"He'll be a child forever," she'd said. "He'll never grow up. Even vampires find that strange."

I'd never thought about that before. If someone was bitten and turned into a vampire when they were young, they'd be stuck at that age for the rest of their lives. I'd tried to imagine what it would be like to be eight years old forever…

"You'll have to invite him over," Mum had said. "We need to check if you're right about him."

"You've invited Bane Larkin for dinner?" April had asked the next day, her eyes wet. "But he put a worm in my hair!"

"It was my mum's idea," I'd said, feeling guilty.

"You've never invited *me* over," April had told me.

I'd felt terrible.

The meal with Bane had been very awkward. First, Mum had shone a torch in his eyes to see if it caused him pain. It hadn't. Second, she'd passed a blue light across his skin to see if it burned him. It didn't.

She'd glowered at me, shaking her head.

I'd been wrong. Bane Larkin wasn't a vampire. He was just a really mean boy.

There was no way I'd make that mistake twice. I didn't want to see that look on Mum's face again. I had to be sure about Dimi before I told her.

I would have to investigate by myself.

Once dinner was over, Mum told me to change into my fighting gear (a black top, a black hoodie and black leggings). I thought we were going to train in the basement as usual but, when I got downstairs, Mum was standing by the front door.

"It took you five and a half minutes to get changed," she

said, tapping her watch. "I was ready in two. You need to be quicker, Henrietta. Much quicker."

"I didn't know you were timing me," I replied, trying to stay polite. "And please call me Etty."

"Vampire hunters can't be styling their hair in the mirror when there's an emergency," she snapped.

"I wasn't doing that!"

"You're right," she said. "Your hair's still tangled and messy."

I drew in a deep breath to stay calm.

Mum laid a hand on my shoulder and smiled. "I'm taking you on your first mission."

Immediately, a rush of excitement flooded my veins. "What will we be doing?" I asked.

"Hunting vampires, of course," she said. "We think there could be a clan of them in town. Another woman's been found dead. That's two in a month."

"What?" I said, my mind struggling to catch up.

"Deidre Salamay was found this morning," Mum answered. "A poisoned knife, the same as Helen."

A poisoned knife... The words rattled in my brain. "Helen was poisoned with a knife?" I said, appalled. "Why didn't you tell me this before?"

"It was confidential," Mum replied. "I know Helen was a friend of Grandma Elsie's, but believe me, Elsie will survive. There isn't a poison strong enough to stop that woman."

I tried not to pull a face. Grandma Elsie's friend had been killed with a knife! I suppressed a shiver. "Why a knife? You said it was vampires. Why didn't they suck her blood?" *And why are they attacking innocent old women?*

"Helen and Deidre's houses were... protected," Mum

replied. "The vampires couldn't get inside, so they laced small knives with poison and threw them through the window. Deidre managed to cut one of them before they got away. There were spots of blood."

I covered my mouth with my hand.

"The blood was black," Mum continued.

Mum's training echoed in my head. *Vampire blood is darker than a human's. When it dries, it's like black tar.*

My hands began to tremble. Deidre Salamay had been attacked by vampires, and the same had happened to Helen. She hadn't died of old age. She'd been murdered. My stomach turned over. I wrapped my arms around myself, trying to keep it together.

Mum didn't seem to notice my distress. "One of the neighbours saw three men leaving Deidre's house last night," she continued eagerly. "The men wore old-fashioned clothes. They were vampires – they had to be."

"Three?" I murmured.

"Yes, Henrietta," she said. "We're heading to Deidre's house. I left sensors there, and tonight someone's set them off. Someone is in Deidre's house right now, and I'll bet it's the one of the vampires. They must have left something behind."

We were going to Deidre's house? Where she'd died, where three vampires had murdered her?

I can't go there!

But there was no time to argue. Mum opened the door and marched out to the car, waving for me to follow her.

I tried to swallow my fear. It didn't work.

Be strong, Etty, I thought as I walked towards the car. *You're a hunter.*

CHAPTER 9

DEIDRE'S HOUSE WAS on the other side of town, near the woods. The roads were dark and empty – no streetlights, no cars and no houses. When Mum stopped the car, we were in the middle of nowhere. She'd parked outside a cottage with ivy crawling up the walls and a short, bushy hedge around the front garden.

"We're here," Mum said. "Take this."

She passed me a white stake. It was made of waxwood (a light but strong wood that doesn't splinter). Then she passed me a flash grenade and a steel chain. Without waiting another moment, she got out of the car and crouched by the front gate of the cottage.

Before I followed her, I pocketed the stake and the grenade, and tied the chain around my waist like a belt.

"The front door's open," Mum whispered once I had caught up with her, "and I see people moving around inside. The vamps are still in there." She squeezed my shoulder. "Follow me."

Keeping low, Mum crept along the cobbled garden path,

and I followed a step behind. Our shoes scraped on the stones. I winced at every sound. Could the vampires hear us? Did they know we were here? Shadows moved behind the windows and voices mumbled quietly.

My heart thudded in my chest.

A few moments later, Mum nudged the front door fully open. I froze but the hallway was empty.

"Remember," Mum said under her breath, "blind them, chain them, then pin them down. Be quick. They're stronger than you, so don't give them a chance to attack."

Blind them, chain them, pin them down. I'd memorised those words since I was a child. I felt inside my pocket for the flash grenade and clasped it tightly.

We continued into the house. It smelled dusty. The lights were off but a swirling white glow came from an open doorway further inside. It was a strange light, like starlight reflected on water.

What are they doing behind that door? I thought.

Mum stopped outside the room and stiffened. "Damn," she muttered.

I peered around her. Had the vampires left? Had we missed them?

It was a living room but all the furniture had been removed apart from a fish tank in the corner. Three elderly women wearing shawls stood in a circle, each wearing a different colour – turquoise, orange and white. A black pot was on the floor between them. Swirling light poured out of it. A fourth woman stood on the opposite side of the room. She wore normal clothes – a plain top and jeans. She was middle-aged, tall and thin, and held something heavy in her arms. All the air vanished from my lungs when I saw what it was – a lifeless body. The body had golden hair, stud earrings and a face I would've recognised anywhere.

April!

I bared my teeth. Mum tried to grab me but I barrelled past her and charged into the room. The woman dressed in white stepped in front of me, but I skittered around her. I jumped over the pot on the floor and landed clumsily. I didn't stop. I reached for April, ready to snatch her up and carry her out of there. Then a chill wind swept across the back of my neck.

"Etty!" a familiar voice said. I stopped in my tracks. A wrinkled hand touched my arm lightly. I drew in a sharp breath as I recognised the woman standing next to me.

Grandma Elsie!

Her turquoise shawl hung loosely around her shoulders and she was wearing so many bracelets and bangles that I was surprised she could lift her arms. "Etty, dear," she said in a gentle voice, "my friend Anna has taken a strength potion tonight." She pointed to the tall, thin woman holding April. Anna shifted so she held April in one arm. Then she raised her fist protectively.

Elsie whispered in my ear, "I wouldn't take my chances, if I were you. Best to step away."

What was going on? Why was Grandma Elsie here? April was unconscious and she didn't seem to care! And what had she meant by 'strength potion'?

Before I knew it, Mum stood at my side. She grabbed my arm. "Etty, come away," she commanded, an edge to her voice. She pulled me backwards – and that's when I noticed the blood. It dripped down April's arm in a thin river.

They've hurt her!

Before Mum could stop me, I darted towards April. Tall, skinny Anna threw out her fist. I tried to dodge her but she caught me in the chest. My ribs juddered, the world tumbled and then I was on my back.

I forced myself to get up. I'd been thrown halfway across the room! Just as this thought occurred to me, Mum drew out her chain. She whipped it at my legs. I caught it in my fist and tugged with all my strength. Mum toppled to the floor.

"Etty!" she shouted. "Stop now!"

April's hurt, I thought. I wasn't going to stop until I'd rescued her.

Anna stood her ground. There wasn't even a hint of muscle on her. How had she managed to throw me across the room like that?

Elsie had mentioned a strength potion…

Mum made a grab for my leg but I somersaulted and landed in front of Elsie. Her bangles jingled as she held up her hands for me to stop.

"If you can get past me, you can take April," she said.

Behind me, I heard Mum approaching. Elsie waved her back.

I took a small step. Elsie raised her hands. At her command, a river of water shot out of the fish tank. I was too shocked to move. The jet pelted towards me. I scrambled backwards and then sideways but the water followed. It struck my hands, wrapped around them and froze like a pair of icy handcuffs. I struggled to keep my balance but another blast struck my ankles and froze them together as well. I hit the floor hard.

Pulling as hard as I could, I tried to break the ice but it held fast. I couldn't get up. I couldn't break free.

No! I thought.

Mum stood over me, scowling.

She hauled me up, stamped on the ice around my ankles so that it shattered, and then held me by the neck of my hoodie. "That was foolish," she muttered under her breath.

A short woman in orange with a matching orange hat had been cowering by the window. Seeing me handcuffed, she straightened her hat and joined the other women in a half-circle around Mum and me. Elsie stood on the left, Anna beside her, next was the woman in the white shawl (whose hair was also pure white), and finally the woman in orange. The ice around my wrists burned my skin and I wriggled my hands to stop them going numb.

"Felicity," the orange-hatted woman said to Mum in a high-pitched voice, "the last time I checked, you were a vampire hunter. Not a witch hunter. Or will you kill anything these days?"

My head snapped up at her words. *Witch?*

"You're witches?" I asked.

"Yes, you silly girl," Orange-hat said.

So witches were real...

It shouldn't have come as such a surprise. Half a tank of water had just flown across the room and handcuffed me.

Beside me, Mum didn't seem a bit surprised by the news. "You already knew," I guessed.

"Of course," she replied.

I didn't know what to say. I was caught between shock and anger.

Witches are real, I thought, the truth finally sinking in. *So Grandma Elsie isn't crazy. She really is a witch. And that means...*

"April's a witch too," I said.

"Yes, dear," Elsie replied, "and she is safe. We're not going to hurt her."

"Then why's she bleeding?" I asked pointedly.

The woman in white stepped forward. The other witches bowed their heads. A deep silence pressed upon the room. This woman was powerful and the others knew it. "Let me introduce myself," she said, her voice deep and reverberating. "My name is Gail. I am the leader of the Brightwood coven."

Mum nodded for me to shake her hand. Gail had a strong handshake for an old woman, clasping mine so tightly it almost hurt.

Once she'd let go, Gail gestured to the other witches. "Patricia is in the orange, Anna is holding April, and you already know Elsie." A muscle twitched in Gail's neck as she spoke Elsie's name. "We're not here to harm April. We're here to make a potion." She pointed to the glowing pot in the middle of the room.

Studying it more closely, I realised it was a cauldron. A gas burner flamed underneath it and white liquid bubbled inside. Gail fixed me with a pair of steely eyes that matched her colourless, white hair. "When a tragic murder takes place, it leaves an energy behind," she said. "Witches can use that energy to make a special kind of potion. That's why we came here. April's blood is needed for the potion. All of our blood is needed. We had to cut her. But the cut will heal quickly."

"But why is April unconscious?" I asked.

"She has not yet received her powers," Patricia said, her orange hat wobbling as she spoke. "April cannot know our true ways until she becomes a true witch."

I was sure I saw Elsie roll her eyes. "April is asleep, that's all," Elsie said. "I gave her a sleeping potion before we arrived. She'll wake up tomorrow morning and she'll never know she was here. And you, my dear, are not going to tell her."

April wasn't hurt, just asleep. My muscles relaxed, and the tension in my neck loosened. But I still felt troubled by the sight of the blood on April's arm.

"So you're allowed to take her blood without her knowing?" I asked, an edge to my voice.

"She is safe," said Gail, "and the potion will help April when it has finished brewing."

"But it's her blood," I said. "She should know what's going on, shouldn't she?"

Did Elsie nod when I said that?

Gail eyed me appraisingly. "You'll learn," she said, "to stay out of witch matters."

Patricia stepped forwards, her orange heels stabbing the carpet. "What I want to know," she said coldly, "is why you hunters are here in Deidre's house in the first place. You force your way in and attack us, and then you start asking us questions like we've committed a crime." She jabbed a finger at Mum. "Felicity, I haven't forgotten what you did all those years ago. I'm surprised you dare to show your face in a witch's house, even if she is dead."

There was an icy silence, colder than the handcuffs on my wrists. What had she meant? What had Mum done?

"We're here," Mum said, "because vampires killed Helen and Deidre and we want to find them."

"You want to spy on us," Patricia said, "that's all. You're—"

"They're not spying," Gail interrupted and Patricia

bowed her head, instantly cowed. "We will help the hunters in any way we can."

"Thank you," Mum said.

Gail graced Mum with an icy look. "We believe there's a new clan in town – six vampires," she told Mum. "They came to Brightwood looking for the Lacuna Gem."

Mum didn't react to the news. The other witches, however, shuffled their feet. Even Elsie folded her arms. *A gem?* I thought, confused. But vampires only cared about blood. Why would they want a gem?

"Six vamps," Mum said. "That's more than I thought. Did they get this gem?"

"Unfortunately, they did," Gail said. "Deidre kept it locked in her cellar, and it's been taken."

"How'd the vamps get inside to take it?" Mum asked.

Gail's lip curled. "Once they'd killed her, the magic ended."

I looked between them, trying to understand what they were talking about. What magic had ended?

Seeing my confused look, Gail spoke. "Witches have many powers that vampires fear. One of them is that we can prevent vampires entering our home unless we give our permission."

Suddenly, it fit into place. "That's why they had to throw a knife to kill Deidre," I said. "They couldn't get inside her house."

Gail nodded. "The vampires laced the knife with poison to make sure it killed her," she said, a look of disgust on her face. "Once Deidre was dead, the magic protecting the house faded and they could take the gem."

"Yes, the gem," Mum said impatiently. "What do the vamps want with it?"

"We don't know," Gail answered. "It isn't a dangerous

object. It's just a black gem. It could be worth something, I suppose."

"But it has power," Anna said in a squeaky voice. Her jeans made her look so out of place among the group of shawled witches, it was hard to believe she was one of the group. Gail tensed at her words, her eyes flashing dangerously as Anna continued. "The gem could be used against witches."

Against witches…?

"Quiet!" snapped Patricia. "Say no more."

Mum leaned closer, her face tense. "I need to know," she said. "The vampires who took it could be planning something."

"Unfortunately," Gail told her, "we cannot share magical information with non-witches."

I waited for Mum to respond, to say something cold or cutting, but nothing came. Was she really going to hold her tongue? They had information we needed!

"But you said you'd help in any way you could," I blurted.

Gail narrowed her eyes. "Not with this," she replied.

I had a feeling I was walking on thin ice, but I didn't care. "Don't you want to find the vampires who did this?" I asked in disbelief. "They killed two witches!"

"We don't reveal witch secrets to outsiders," Gail said, her tone finite. "Now it's time for you to leave." She nodded to Elsie. With a wave of Elsie's hand, the ice around my wrists melted to water and floated back into the fish tank. The blood rushed into my fingers and I flexed them to get the feeling back.

Scowling, Mum muttered a goodbye and swept out of the room. Before I left, I glanced over my shoulder. Grandma Elsie smiled at me warmly, the glow from the cauldron illuminating her face. Gail had already turned away. Patricia glared. I managed to form a thin smile and then slipped out.

That night, I lay in bed, wide awake. I thought about April's grandma. She wasn't crazy after all.

All this time, I'd thought vampires were the only supernatural things in the world. But it turned out a whole bunch of witches were living in Brightwood. Even Deidre and Helen had been witches.

That's what got them killed, I thought.

Deidre had been keeping the Lacuna Gem in her cellar. Had she been protecting it? Had she known the vampires were coming?

I shivered. The clan had poisoned her, broken into her house and stolen the gem. I rubbed my forehead. It didn't make sense. Why would a vampire clan come all the way to Brightwood to steal a magical gem?

Anna said it could be used against witches. Are they planning to attack the coven?

Whatever the vampires wanted to use it for, it couldn't be good.

I brushed the skin on my hand where it had been burned by April's ring. There wasn't even a mark there now.

April's a witch, I thought, clutching my pillow.

I had to tell her what I'd found out. I just didn't know how to do it.

CHAPTER 10

THE NEXT DAY, I walked nervously into class. April was in her usual seat at the back, fiddling with her ring. When she saw me, she smiled. She'd styled her blonde hair into ringlets and her earrings were silver moons. She was wearing her summer dress and I could see the cut on her arm from last night.

I tried to smile but I kept thinking about what had happened at Deidre's house. Grandma Elsie had put April to sleep, cut her, and taken her blood. April had helped make a potion and she didn't even know it. How was I going to tell her the truth? There was no good way to do it without revealing I was a vampire hunter. Mum would kill me if I did that. And, anyway, I wasn't sure I wanted April to know the truth about me. She was the one friend I'd managed to keep over the years. Despite spending most of my younger years picking fights with people, April had stuck by me. I didn't want to scare her off now.

"I'm sorry I got mad at you yesterday," she said the moment I sat down. "I just felt bad about leaving Dimi."

The guilt that had been building up inside me tripled in

size. "Oh, yeah, I'm sorry too," I replied, hardly able to look at her. "I did act a bit strangely."

She looked like she was going to say more but then Miss Gravel started to take the register. After that, it was maths, and we were given a lecture about area and perimeter. I listened as best I could (after all, I enjoyed maths way more than English), but when Miss Gravel turned to write on the board, all I could think about was the cut on April's arm and the blood that had dripped from it.

Miss Gravel set us questions to answer. While we worked, April's eyebrows drew closer and closer together. "I woke up with a really bad headache today," she said once we'd completed a particularly tricky problem. "Grandma told me I'd slept too long, but I think she was lying."

I didn't say anything. I felt rotten.

I'd have a headache too if someone gave me a sleeping potion and took some of my blood.

"I always know when Grandma's keeping something from me," April continued. "It's strange. I woke up with a cut on my arm, and I have no idea how it got there. But I'm sure I remember something – people fighting. And I think you were there."

My insides twisted into a knot. "You must have dreamt it," I lied, keeping my eyes fixed on the desk.

"Etty, I know it sounds mad, but do you think I could be a witch?" she asked. "Gran keeps telling me it's true – and there's something weird about this ring. Ever since I put it on, I've had this odd feeling."

She waited for an answer, her forehead creased.

"I… I don't know," I said. "Try not to worry about it."

At that moment, the bell rang for break. I let out a breath

as I cleared our desk, but I could feel April watching me. On the other side of the room, Dimi stood alone at his desk.

April had noticed too. "We have to apologise to him," she said. "He looked really sad after we ran off and left him yesterday."

I shuddered. "No," I said, trying to keep my voice calm. "I think we should just stay away from him. We don't want to upset him again. He's clearly very sensitive."

"Sensitive?" April replied incredulously. "You knocked his drink on the floor and then we ran off! Of course he got upset! We have to say sorry."

What was I going to say? I couldn't let her apologise to Dimi. What if they became friends? He was a vampire! But she'd think I was heartless if I did nothing.

"Fine," I replied. "I'll talk to him later."

"Great! We can do it together."

"No!" I said, my voice harsher than I'd intended, but April was already walking over to Dimi.

My insides shrivelled. Before I knew what was happening, Dimi was following us to the playground like a rabbit caught in headlights.

It was worse than awkward. Dimi wrung his hands and barely spoke for the whole break. We sat at a picnic bench in the glorious sunshine, in complete silence. April made a valiant effort to get us talking, but all I kept thinking about were Vladimir's huge, black eyes behind those sunglasses. How many humans had he bitten? How much blood had he drunk?

By the time we were called back inside, I hoped April had given up on being Dimi's friend. However, as we climbed the stairs to the first floor, I caught Dimi whispering under his breath: "Stop being so nervous. Just say something. Say something."

"A-April," Dimi said out loud. His eyes widened as if he'd surprised himself. "Thanks for hanging out with me."

April grinned, clearly pleased. "You're welcome, Dimi," she said. "I'm sorry about what happened yesterday at lunch. I wanted to make it up to you." She waited for me to say something, and then pinched my arm.

I wished I could tell her that I didn't want to apologise to him because he was a bloodsucking vampire. Instead, I shrugged. Apparently this wasn't what April had been hoping for. She shook her head at me as we walked into class.

I was in a foul mood the rest of the morning. Dimi, the vampire, was becoming April's friend and I didn't know what to do about it – apart from stab him through the heart.

At lunch, we sat together in the hall with its chipped tables and food-covered floor. The dinner ladies shuffled around us, checking lunches and shushing pupils who were being too loud. Their efforts were in vain – the hall was as noisy and chaotic as ever. The kids at the table next to us looked close to breaking into a fight over a spilled packet of crisps.

Dimi got out his carrot sticks and started chomping away. With every bite, I imagined him sinking his teeth into someone's neck. He took a sip from his bottle, which was filled with red liquid again, and I tried to ignore the sick feeling in my stomach.

"I-I love carrots," he said and then he blushed. "S-sorry, that was a weird thing to say…"

I narrowed my eyes at him.

"I love chocolate," April said, holding up three chocolate bars. "Actually, I like anything with lots of sugar in it."

"I'm not allowed to eat too much sugar," Dimi said. "Dad makes me eat vegetables. I-I actually really like them now. Especially carrots."

"You're like Etty," April said. "She's not allowed sugar either."

"My mum thinks sugar's evil," I said. "But I think there are more evil things around." I glared at Dimi until his cheeks flamed.

"Well, my grandma doesn't care about sugar," April said. "She sort of lets me eat what I want."

"What do your parents say?" Dimi asked her.

April didn't answer for a moment. "They don't say anything," she said. "They died when I was young. I don't remember them."

I wanted to kick Dimi under the table.

Dimi seemed to shrink into his chair. "I-I'm sorry."

"That's okay," April said with a reassuring smile. "Grandma can be a bit strange, but she's the best cook in the world. I really don't have it that bad."

"Your grandma sounds like my tutor – Maggie," Dimi replied. "Maggie cooked the nicest pizzas. She was always giving me extra portions because she thought I was too thin."

"Do you miss her?" April asked.

"Y-yes," he said. "I used to spend every day with her. It's not the same now I'm at school and she doesn't live with us any more. Dad c-can't cook at all. He even burns toast."

April chuckled and I squeezed my sandwich so hard, butter oozed out the sides.

"Whenever I missed my mum," Dimi said, "Maggie used

to say 'family is blood'. She'd tell me 'your mother is the blood inside you, Dimi, flowing through you'. I know it's silly but, even though she's gone, I still feel like I have part of my mum with me."

He's a good actor, I thought. *He almost made me believe that fake story.*

My stomach churned. He really was pure evil. All that stuff about family and blood – it was all rubbish. I just wished I knew why he was trying to be April's friend.

"Oh no!" April said. She shut her lunchbox and shoved it into her bag. "I forgot, I have to go to orchestra. I'm running late."

"Y-you're leaving us?" Dimi asked, his voice going very high-pitched.

She was going to make us spend the rest of lunch together by ourselves? Was she mad?

"Well, you could come with me," she suggested.

"Yes!" we both said at once.

The music room had instruments hanging on the walls, dangling from the ceiling and stacked on shelves in the corners. Everywhere you looked, there was a guitar or a keyboard. April had forgotten her violin and so she took one off a shelf and then joined the other students. They'd already started playing, some on flutes, some on recorders. There were even a few trumpets. Mr Briggs (the ancient, hump-backed music teacher) conducted them with his baton.

"You're just in time, April," he croaked in his withered voice. "Your solo's coming up."

Dimi and I perched on stools at the back of the room. We'd just sat down when the instruments stopped playing – all except one. I leaned forward and grinned. Beside me, Dimi's eyes widened and he put his hands to his mouth.

"She's amazing," he whispered.

"I know," I replied.

April shut her eyes as she played. Her fingers moved over the strings, her bow gliding up and down. Her music drifted through the room like a lullaby. I recognised the piece: she'd played it to me before.

The other players shuffled, waiting for their cue to join in.

"I-I could dance to this," Dimi said. "It sounds like the music Maggie used to play."

I shushed him. "I'm trying to listen."

He turned pink and was silent.

When Mr Briggs called an end to practice, April put the violin back and we walked to class.

"Y-you were incredible," Dimi said. "I w-wish I could play an instrument."

April beamed. "Thanks, Dimi."

"Maggie plays piano," he said. "She played the best music I've ever heard. But you're just as good and she's been doing it for years!"

"Wow, do you really think so?" April said, practically glowing, her hair sparking with excitement.

"Yeah, y-you're really gifted!"

I let them carry on ahead of me. April and Dimi chatted away as they walked along the corridor. My heart sank.

I love your music, I thought. *I just don't need to say it because it's obvious.*

Did Dimi really think April's music was good? Vampires didn't care about things like that. All they cared about was... blood.

I shuddered.

At the end of the day, April walked out of school with me, her blonde hair shimmering in the sun. We must have looked like such opposites. She shone with golden light, whereas I was hard and cold. Even my eyes were pale grey – there was no warmth in them.

She must have looked like a perfect meal for a vampire.

I'm not going to let Dimi have her.

Her ring reflected the sunlight, gleaming like her hair. The triangular yellow stone caught my eye. I thought of the crystals her grandma wore.

The Lacuna Gem. The witches wouldn't tell us what it was, but perhaps Elsie had already told April. If I knew what it did, maybe I could figure out why the vampires were looking for it.

"April," I said, trying to keep my voice light, "has your grandma ever talked about gems?"

"Gems?" April said. "Well, yeah. She talks about crystals and gems a lot."

"Black gems?" I asked.

"I don't think so," she said, narrowing her eyes. She stopped walking, but the breeze still caught in her hair. "Why?"

"No reason," I replied.

She didn't move. She watched me, waiting expectantly for a proper answer. Quickly, I tried to come up with an excuse. "I was… thinking about getting a necklace. I thought black would be a good colour." It was a terrible lie.

April folded her arms. She knew I didn't like jewellery.

It was obvious she didn't believe me. I couldn't blame her. "Etty," she said, "if you know something…"

This was the moment. I should reveal the truth. But how could I explain about vampires and witches and gems without saying I was a hunter? "No," I said at last, "I don't know anything."

Mum didn't make it home for dinner that night. Dad had cooked fajitas and we ate until we were stuffed. Afterwards, he brought out ice cream.

"Don't tell your mother," he said, scooping a big portion into a bowl.

"I shouldn't…"

He plonked the bowl in front of me and handed me the spoon. "It's toffee," he said. "Your favourite."

Like criminals, we ate our ice cream, keeping a look-out in case Mum walked in. We needn't have bothered. She didn't show up until we'd finished washing up.

She marched into the kitchen, grabbed a fajita wrap and planted a quick kiss on Dad's cheek. "Henrietta, get changed," she said. "We have another mission."

Thinking of last night's catastrophe, I flinched.

"Don't worry, there won't be any witches," she said. "We need more information on the vampire clan. I'm taking you to the place vampires like to hang out."

"Where?" I asked.

"The graveyard," she said with a dark smile.

CHAPTER 11

"STAY WITH ME at all times," Mum told me as we got out of the car. It was dark and there was only one streetlight nearby.

The graveyard was in the centre of Brightwood, and contained rows and rows of graves. According to April, it was one of the biggest graveyards in England. *Great,* I thought, *the vampires must really love it here.*

In front of us stood St Luke's Church, with its tall towers and grimy bricks. People called it haunted and I could see why: it was menacing in the darkness. In fact, the whole place was spooky. The church had gargoyles on each corner of the roof, and many of its windows were boarded up.

Mum walked towards the graveyard, putting her finger to her lips as we passed through the rusty gates. My heart started to race. The gravestones and shadows creeped me out. I didn't like the thought that there were dead people beneath my feet.

Mum stopped. Her black leather jacket shone in the pale moonlight, as did her glossy black hair, which was pulled into a tight ponytail. "I knew it," she whispered. "He's here again."

"Who?" I asked.

"I've been watching the graveyard ever since Helen's death. Each time I've come, I've seen the same vampire. I thought he might be here tonight – and I was right. I can smell him."

"I can't smell anything," I said.

She tutted. "You're a vampire hunter! Your senses are stronger than a normal human. When I was your age, I could smell a vampire from a mile away."

I sniffed at the air. Nothing.

"Don't worry," she said. "Your powers should appear eventually…"

She carried on walking.

What did that mean? Was there a chance that I wouldn't get my powers? I followed her, thinking about what she'd said as I stepped between the mossy gravestones. She hadn't sounded very confident.

Maybe she's right. Maybe my powers will never come. I've never beaten her in training. I have no special hunter senses. What if I'm not a hunter? I definitely don't feel like one right now.

Mum didn't even seem bothered by the fact that people from our town had been killed. In fact, she strode ahead of me like she couldn't wait to find out more. All I could think about were the two old women who were dead.

The further we walked, the darker the graveyard became. All the while, I tried not to think about Helen and Deidre or my lack of hunter talent. The tombstones were more cracked here. Some of them had completely crumbled.

"Why do vampires hang around in places like this?" I asked.

"The dead give them power," she replied, "and grave-yards are full of the dead."

She opened her mouth to say more but then something caught her eye and she ducked down behind a gravestone, pulling me with her.

Out of the shadows walked a man. His hair was black but the top of his head was bald. His skin was pale but it also had red patches here and there, as if he had a rash. His clothes were dirty, and I didn't need special hunter senses to smell him. He stank of cabbage. He was nothing like the vampires I'd seen in pictures and films. He was plump, and for some reason he reminded me of a fat rat.

Mum gestured for me to stay where I was. My heart thudded in my chest as she stood up and walked towards the vampire. She didn't show a hint of fear. I stayed hidden behind the gravestone.

"Good evening," she said politely when the vampire saw her. "My name is Felicity."

"A delicious name!" he said, sniffing his crusty fingers. He had a squeaky voice to match his ratty face. "I am Raif. Just out for a walk!" His face cracked into a wide smile that revealed gleaming white teeth. He looked mad.

"Your teeth are almost perfect," Mum said, an edge to her voice.

"I brush twice a day," he replied.

"They're so white, they almost glow in the dark," she said.

He backed away a step. "I take good care of them."

"And what about your *fangs*?"

She threw out her arm. A stake shot out of her sleeve and

soared towards him. I was sure it would hit him but, at the last moment, he ducked out of the way. He stood up again, his face filled with terror and rage.

"Vampire hunter!" Raif shouted. Without warning, he bounded towards Mum. She leapt away but he was fast – faster than I could've imagined. The two of them danced around each other, ducking and dodging. Mum shot towards him like a snake and he dropped to the ground to avoid her. He kicked at her ankle but she managed to jump out of the way just in time, then leapt forward and pounced on him. In the blink of an eye, he was pinned underneath her. She smirked as she held a wooden stake to his chest.

Raif whimpered in fear.

"Tell me about the vampire clan," Mum demanded. "I know there's a group of them in town."

"I won't tell you anything!"

"Two women have been killed!" she shouted and she pressed the stake harder to his chest. "Talk!"

"Okay! Okay!" he said. "I followed the clan to Brightwood. I wanted to join them. There are six of them. Some of them are old, very old. They're looking for something – a gem."

"What does it do? Why do they want it?"

"I don't know, I swear!"

"They killed two witches to get that gem!" Mum snarled. "It must do something powerful!"

"I told you, I don't know!"

She sighed and then slammed him against the dirt. "You had a lot of nerve coming here," she said. "I don't allow vampires in my town."

"I've been here for weeks!" he retorted angrily. "You haven't kept me out!"

"Brightwood is off-limits to scum like you," she breathed.

"That's what you think!" he said.

"What do you mean?"

Raif chuckled madly. "There's been a vampire here for years!" he yelled but then his hand flew to his mouth.

"What did you say?" Mum asked.

"N-nothing," he muttered.

Mum pulled out a flash grenade from her jacket. "Speak, or I'll set this off in front of your face. You'll be blinded for days."

"No, please don't!" he yelped.

"Then tell me what you know."

"A powerful vampire has lived here for years," he said. "The witches say he will be stronger and crueller than any other vampire in the world. And he's been here, under your nose, the whole time. They say he will lead an army. I pray to him at night. He's my lord! I'd do anything to meet him, just once!"

"And what makes this 'vampire' so powerful?" Mum asked as if she didn't believe a word Raif had said.

"I don't know," he replied. "All I know for sure is that he wasn't bitten like most of us. He was born a vampire."

Born a vampire? I raised my eyebrows. Mum had said there were hardly any vampires like that in the whole world.

"There are two types," she'd once told me. "The born and the bitten. Nearly all the vampires you'll meet are bitten – they're strong and fast. But born vampires are stronger and faster. Even when they're young, born vampires are a threat."

A shadow had passed across her face. "Pray you never have to fight one."

Born vampires were vampire royalty, like kings and queens. They were the original vampires – the first ones to ever walk on Earth. They could even have children together and create more born vampires! Their children grew from babies just the same as humans – except, once they were adults, they stopped ageing and lived forever.

Bitten vampires, on the other hand, didn't grow and they couldn't have children. They were just humans who'd been infected with vampire venom. Once they turned, they were stuck at their current age forever, even if they were only a toddler. The bitten were a weaker, less pure form of vampire, but still deadly.

If there really was a born vampire living in Brightwood, we were all in danger.

Mum had gone pale.

"Nonsense," she said. "There's no vampire living in my town, especially not a born one. I would have known if there was. You've made it up."

"He's real!" Raif spat. "I know a witch from my homeland. She told me about him."

"Then what's his name?"

Raif shook his head.

"If you don't tell me," Mum said in a dangerous voice, "I'll take this stake and stab it through your heart."

I held tightly to the gravestone. *Stab him? She can't! We never kill vampires. The rules say we must capture them and send them to Traxis.*

"You're going to kill me?" Raif said, his eyes wide.

"Tell me the vampire's name."

"His name is…"

"Speak!"

"His name is Vladimir! Vladimir Nox!"

My heart stopped.

Vladimir!

It couldn't be Dimi, surely?

He was going to be the strongest, cruellest vampire in the world?

No way!

CHAPTER 12

I COULD HARDLY believe it. Dimi, the stammering, nervous boy with the purple lunchbox was going to be the strongest vampire in the world? How had Raif known? He'd said something about the witches. He'd made it sound like there was some sort of prophecy about Dimi…

I tried to imagine Dimi leading an army of vampires, dressed up as a vampire lord. I couldn't.

He's always so nervous! I thought. *Is it all just an act? Does he stammer and make himself look nervous to cover up his powers?*

I clutched the gravestone with sweaty hands.

All I wanted to do was leave. But, instead of letting Raif go, Mum raised the stake above her head. She was going to stab him with it! If the wood hit his heart, it would kill him. He would turn to dust!

"I've told you everything!" the ratty vampire shrieked.

She wasn't listening.

Without thinking, I stood up and stepped forward. "Stop!"

Mum looked at me, distracted. Grabbing his chance,

Raif shoved her away. Before she could stop him, he had disappeared into the shadows.

Mum turned to face me. If looks could kill, I'd be dead. She threw the stake across the graveyard and kicked the ground in anger, then turned and marched back to the car.

We didn't talk as she drove us home. Her hands gripped the steering wheel as if she wanted to strangle it, her knuckles white.

When we walked into the house, she slammed the door and marched upstairs.

"Wait!" I called after her. "I'm sorry. I didn't mean to—"

"You're *sorry*?" she interrupted. "You let a dangerous vampire escape. He could hurt innocent people."

"I thought you were going to kill him."

"I was," she said fiercely. "Sometimes we have to do terrible things. That's what hunters do."

"I don't want to kill anyone."

"Then you will never be a hunter."

Her words hit me like a punch.

I thought she was going to turn away, but then she spoke again. "Henrietta, I should be focused on finding the vampire clan. For all we know, the gem they were after is dangerous. But you let Raif escape – and now I have to worry about him hurting someone."

"What about Di- Vladimir?" I said.

"He's not real," she replied, "just someone Raif made up in his unhinged mind." She carried on upstairs.

"Wait," I said. "There's something I need to tell you."

She paused, her body tense. "Yes?" she said. "Spit it out, Henrietta."

I took a deep breath. I had to tell her about Dimi. She

thought he wasn't real. She didn't know he was in my class at school. If she knew who he was, she'd be able to capture him and send him back to Traxis before he could hurt anyone.

"It's about Vladimir," I said.

She stared at me, waiting.

"I think…" My voice trailed off. I knew I should tell her. She had to know the truth – but I kept seeing her with that wooden stake in her hand. She would've killed the vampire in the graveyard if I hadn't distracted her. Would she do the same to Dimi?

I wanted him to be sent away. I wanted him in prison. After all, he was a vampire who drank human blood. But I didn't want him *dead*.

"What is it, Henrietta?" Mum asked impatiently.

I opened my mouth to tell her, but I couldn't get the words to come out. They were stuck in my throat.

"Henrietta?"

I couldn't do it.

She sighed. "If you're worried about this Vladimir Nox, then don't be," she said. "Worry about the gem and the clan of vampires instead."

She continued upstairs without looking back.

The moment I got into bed, I squeezed my eyes shut and tried not to think about what I'd done. I'd never kept such a big secret from Mum before.

What if Dimi hurt someone?

Maybe I could capture him myself. I'd never done it before, but I was a hunter and I knew how. I'd just need a stake and a prison car from Hunters Corp. I'd back him into a corner, blind him with a flash grenade and then tie his hands with chains.

I can't do it yet, though. I need more time to figure out a proper plan. I can't go setting off grenades at school.

Dimi wasn't the only thing on my mind either. I kept thinking about the lies I'd told April.

What was she going to do when she found out the truth?

I squeezed my eyes shut, trying to get to sleep.

CHAPTER 13

THE NEXT DAY, Dad took me to school. I hadn't seen Mum. Apparently, she left early on 'hunter business', but I had a feeling she was still mad at me.

"You're quiet," Dad said as he drove. "What's up, Etty?"

I fiddled with a button on my shirt. "Last night, when I was out with Mum, I did something I wasn't supposed to."

"Your mother can be hard on you," he said gently, "but it's only because she loves you and she doesn't want you to get hurt. Etty, you'll become a great hunter. I'm sure of it."

I thought about what Mum had said about hunters. *Sometimes we have to do terrible things.* Was she right? Would I have to kill a vampire one day?

"Dad," I said. "Do you think it's ever okay to hurt someone… if it's to protect people you care about?"

"That's a difficult question, Etty," he replied, "but I think there's always a way to protect the ones we love without hurting anyone. Why do you ask?"

"Oh, no reason," I replied.

He kissed me goodbye when we arrived at the school

gates. I took a deep breath as I walked inside. Once I stepped into class, I glanced around for Vladimir.

My stomach lurched when I saw him sitting in the front row. He was wearing his purple bowtie with matching purple-rimmed sunglasses. It was difficult to keep my expression calm.

After taking the register, Miss Gravel made us change for PE and, in our shorts and T-shirts, we walked down to the hall. It was the oldest part of the school, with thickly varnished wooden floors and unpainted brick walls.

"Our first sport this year," Miss Gravel said, "is dance."

A few of the boys sniggered. I tried not to roll my eyes. When were we going to do some karate or boxing? I was actually good at those things! April, meanwhile, was bouncing on the balls of her feet.

Miss Gravel split us into twos and told us to stand opposite each other. April's shoulders slumped when she found out she was paired with Bane Larkin. Finally, my name was called out. My partner was Vladimir. My heart sank.

I stood opposite him. His PE clothes were black, which made his skin look even paler.

He smiled shyly.

You can't fool me, I thought. *I know you what you are.*

Raif's words echoed in my head. *I pray to him at night. He's my lord!*

Dimi might be pretending to be innocent and kind, but I wasn't going to let my guard down around him. The witches said he would become the cruellest vampire in the world. I sent him my nastiest cold, hard stare.

Miss Gravel told us to take it in turns to mirror our partner's movements. Slowly, Dimi raised his arms and twirled them elegantly in the air. A moment later, he lifted his leg up and spun on one foot. My mouth dropped open. He was so graceful. He moved like a ballet dancer. I tried to mirror him, but I couldn't get my arms to move so fluidly or my leg to lift so high. Then, when I tried to spin around, I stumbled and almost fell.

The rest of the class had started to notice Dimi's dancing, and some of the boys were gazing at him in amazement. Even Miss Gravel was astounded. Bane Larkin, however, snorted with laughter.

"Look!" he shouted. "It's a fairy!"

Dimi stopped. Apparently, he hadn't realised everyone was staring at him. He blushed.

"Carry on!" Miss Gravel shouted. "All of you!"

This time it was Dimi's turn to copy me. I had an idea. I stretched out my hand towards him and he mirrored my movement. Our hands moved closer and closer. Finally, our fingertips touched. His were icy cold, like metal in winter.

"Your hands are freezing," I said.

"I-I'm always cold," he replied.

He sounded so nervous. The way his lips twitched seemed so genuine. Even his fingers shook slightly where they met mine.

I pulled my hands back so we no longer touched. "So where do you live?" I asked as I performed some basic hand movements for him to copy.

"Um, by the cliffs near the beach," he replied.

In the rich part of town. That made sense. If he really was a born vampire, that meant his dad was one too. And vampires like that would want to live somewhere luxurious.

"Have you always lived in Brightwood?" I asked.

"Y-yes," he replied, "but my dad is f-from Romania."

"What about your mum?"

"She was born here in England, I think," he said. "Dad doesn't talk about her much."

I wondered if she was a vampire too. "Did your mum have the same problem with her eyes?" I asked, gesturing towards his sunglasses.

At that moment, Miss Gravel called an end to the lesson and I never heard the answer to my question. We headed back upstairs to get changed.

In the corridor, something tugged on the back of my T-shirt. Spinning around, I saw it was Vladimir.

"Y-you forgot your water bottle," he said, smiling.

My heart raced. Everyone else was back in the classroom. We were alone. Trying not to panic, I pulled my T-shirt out of his grip and backed away.

"What's wrong?" he asked.

"Nothing. I…"

"Etty?" he said as I continued to step backwards.

I hurried into the classroom, my blood as cold as a vampire's.

Always be on your guard, Mum's voice rang in my head. *Never let yourself be alone with a vampire unless you have a plan.*

I needed to be more careful.

CHAPTER 14

WHEN DIMI CAME back into class, I wanted to shrink down into my chair.

I saw something fly across the room and hit him on the back of the head. It was a scrunched-up ball of paper. When he turned around, Bane Larkin smiled nastily at him.

April gripped my arm. "Do you remember when Bane put a worm in my lunchbox?" she asked.

I nodded.

"He's doing the same thing to Dimi," she continued. "He's bullying him. He's picking on him because he's different."

"Yes, he is different," I muttered coolly.

She frowned. "You should try to make friends with him," she said. "He's really sweet."

"That's not a good idea. Trust me."

"Why don't you like him?" April asked. "You've not exactly been friendly."

I didn't know what to say. My mouth hung open. "He's... weird."

"How can you say that?" she asked. "He's a bit different, but so what? I don't care that he likes purple and that he wears a bowtie and that he can ballet dance! And I didn't think you would care either."

I met her eyes. "Stay away from him, April."

"No," she replied, shocked. "He's lonely and he needs a friend."

"He's not lonely," I said. "Stay away from him."

"I won't."

I clenched my fists, trying to think of something to say. I couldn't let her become his friend and spend time alone with him.

"Fine," I said at last, "then you'll have to choose between us. Me or him."

Before she could answer, Miss Gravel noticed us talking and told us to pay attention.

After that, we didn't speak to each other. At the end of the lesson, April stormed off before I had a chance to stop her. I was about to follow so that we could talk but I stopped myself. I didn't know what to say. I shouldn't have asked her to choose between Dimi and me. I just didn't know what else to do.

I rested my forehead against the desk and squeezed my eyes shut. When I opened them, the classroom was empty. I breathed a sigh of relief.

I headed out of class but my relief vanished when I caught sight of Dimi waiting in the corridor. A second later, I realised he wasn't alone – and he wasn't waiting for me. Bane Larkin was holding Dimi's purple lunchbox out of his reach, and Dimi was trying to get it back.

The two of them looked so alike, with the same black

hair and pale skin, except Bane was taller and bulkier and his face was wider.

"Come and get your lunchbox, fairy!" Bane grunted. He shoved Dimi in the chest and laughed when the vampire boy fell to the floor.

I had to do something. If Bane carried on making Dimi angry, he could end up with a set of fangs in his neck! I had to stop him.

Suddenly, Miss Gravel came around the corner. She saw the boys and told them to take their lunches to the hall. Bane helped Dimi to his feet, pretending to be friendly, and they disappeared down the staircase. Bane gripped Dimi's shoulder – I could tell he was holding it too tightly.

I went to follow them, but Miss Gravel called me back. "Etty," she said, pushing her glasses higher on her nose, "can I talk to you?"

She told me she wasn't happy about my chatting in class. While I listened, I kept glancing in the direction the two boys had just gone, a horrible feeling in my stomach.

When Miss Gravel had finished telling me off, I apologised and said that I wouldn't do it again (with my fingers crossed behind my back) and then hurried downstairs.

Frantically, I searched the lunch hall but there was no sign of them. Even April was nowhere to be found. I checked the field and the playground, I checked the toilets, and then I retraced my steps and checked them all again. I couldn't find them. It was as if they'd vanished.

I'd been so busy looking that when the bell rang for the end of lunch, I remembered I hadn't eaten anything.

Nervously, I walked into class. My heart sank when I saw April. She wasn't sitting in her usual place. She was in the front row next to Vladimir. So she had made a choice. She'd chosen him.

Dimi had switched his purple sunglasses for a plain black pair. He was whispering to April.

Sighing, I went to my seat and tried to ignore the empty chair next to me. I couldn't help my eyes drifting towards April and Dimi, however. Watching them chatting, smiling, laughing with each other was like having a hammer strike me in the chest.

Miss Gravel cleared her throat to take the register. It was when she called Bane's name that I noticed something was wrong.

He wasn't here.

"Bane?" she said again. She waited. "Has anyone seen Bane?"

No one answered.

Her brow creased but she carried on taking the register. While the rest of the class quietly read their books, I kept my eyes on the door, waiting for Bane to walk in. He didn't.

By the end of the day, he still hadn't turned up. Miss Gravel had rung the office several times and the head teacher had come into the classroom twice to check where he was. It seemed that Bane had disappeared.

I tried not to show the panic rushing through me.

The last time I'd seen Bane, he'd been with Vladimir. He'd been teasing him. He'd pushed him. And now Bane had vanished.

Dimi must have done something to Bane. Maybe he'd attacked him and drunk his blood...

It's all my fault. I should've told Mum about Dimi last night! She could've stopped this.

And now he was hanging around with April. What if something happened to her?

I watched them constantly, even on the way out of school. At the least sign of trouble, I was ready to step in. But nothing happened. They waved goodbye to each other and April made her way over to Elsie's car. Dimi carried on walking up the road.

The police were outside, red and blue lights flashing. Policemen were interviewing teachers, talking to parents. As soon as Dad's truck pulled up, I climbed in and told him we had to get home fast. I needed to talk to Mum.

"Sweetheart," he said softly, "I wanted to wait till we were home."

"What?" I asked. "What is it?"

"It's your mum," he said carefully. "She... she never came back from her mission this morning." He stroked my hair and then pulled me into a hug.

"Dad," I said, my voice shaking, "where is she?"

"I don't know, Etty. I'm afraid... I'm afraid she's been taken."

"Taken?"

"By vampires."

All of a sudden, I couldn't breathe.

Taken!

Mum was gone. It took several moments for it to sink in. Where was she? Was she okay? Was she... alive?

There was a vampire in my class and one of my classmates had disappeared. And I was on my own.

Mum, I need you.

CHAPTER 15

DAD SAT AT the kitchen table staring at the salt and pepper shakers. He'd been doing that for the past ten minutes. I, on the other hand, had been pacing up and down. I couldn't sit still. I kept thinking about Mum and remembering the argument we'd had last night. I'd let the vampire in the graveyard escape and then I hadn't said anything about Vladimir. Now he'd done something to Bane and the one person who could help me stop him was gone.

She's gone. The thought made me wince.

"We have to find her," I said at last. "What was her mission this morning? Where did she go?"

Dad's eyes were watery. "She didn't say. I contacted Hunters Corp but they wouldn't tell me much. They don't like outsiders knowing their business. They just said they're looking for her and not to call the police."

"What if I spoke to them?" I suggested. "I'm a hunter. They might tell me what they know."

"You're not a full hunter yet," he said, "but there might be another way to find out where she went." He stood up and headed into the hall. "I can't get in touch with her. I think her phone's been destroyed. But she might have left something behind…" He slid open the secret panel and typed a code into the keypad.

To my surprise, the basement door clicked open.

"You know the code?" I asked.

"I watched your mum typing it in when she wasn't looking."

I raised my eyebrows. "You spied on her?"

He didn't answer. The floor creaked as he walked down the steps. I followed him. It felt strange to be in here without Mum. Dad looked out of place among the training equipment, and he glanced over at the wall of weapons with concern. I realised that he had never been down here before.

He tried to open one of the cupboards but it was locked as usual. My eyes were drawn towards the oldest-looking cabinet. It was made of polished mahogany. I'd always wondered what was inside.

Dad noticed what I was staring at. He tried to open it, but it was locked like all the others. "There must be something around here that can tell us where she is," he said quietly.

Desperate, I grabbed a sword off the wall and carried it over to the cabinet.

"Be careful," Dad said.

I slid the tip of the sword into the gap between the cabinet doors and wrenched them open, cracking the wood and sending splinters flying. The moment I saw what was inside, I gasped.

There were bottles and herbs and ancient-looking books. There was even an old cauldron, just like the one I'd seen Elsie and the other witches using in Deidre's living room.

"What is all this?" I asked.

"Those things belonged to a close friend of your mother's," he said, his voice sad. "I didn't know your mum had kept them."

"What friend?" I asked. "I didn't think Mum had any friends."

I touched the cauldron. It was rough, the metal rusted in places. I traced my fingers over the herbs.

"You didn't know her," Dad replied. "She died when you were young."

"Mum's friend was a witch, wasn't she?" I guessed.

"Yes," he answered. "Your mum's friend was a witch. Her name was Lisa. They were close friends for years and then… Her death changed your mother."

"How did she die?" I asked.

"That's a story for your mother to tell," he replied.

"It had something to do with vampires, didn't it?" I ventured.

He didn't answer.

Mum's friend had been a witch. But, for some reason, she'd died. It made me think of April. What would I do if something happened to her? I didn't even want to think about it.

Is that why Mum had never told me about witches? Was it too painful?

"None of this stuff can help us," Dad said. "These are magical items. Only a witch can use them."

With that, he shut the cabinet as if he was closing a door on the past. He took the sword from my hand and went to break open a chest. While his back was turned, I silently reopened the cabinet and riffled through the pages of the books inside. One of them caught my eye. It contained several pages with pictures of necklaces and crystals. Thankfully it was a thin book, so I was able to shove it into the waistband of my trousers.

As the night wore on, we carried on searching the basement, breaking into every cupboard and every drawer. Inside one of the chests, I found a stack of papers. One piece of paper bore the words *Hunters Corp.* It had a phone number on it! While Dad wasn't paying attention, I stuffed the paper in my pocket.

Eventually, Dad slumped back against a pile of books and let out a sigh. There was nothing down here. Mum had left no clues to tell us where she'd gone.

Dad called me over to him and we sat together among the mess of papers and weapons and books.

"She'll be okay," he said, wrapping his arm around me. "Your mum is as tough as old boots. Nothing frightens her."

His eyes glistened.

"We have to find her," I whispered. I just wished I knew how. What if she was hurt? What if she wasn't alive?

I clutched at my throat.

Stop it, I told myself harshly. *This isn't helping.*

I had to do something useful. I couldn't mope around like this – Mum would never forgive me. There was something important I had to do. I'd wanted Mum's help before, but now she wasn't here. I'd have to do it myself.

Bane had vanished. Someone had hurt him and I was sure I knew who that someone was.

Vladimir Nox.

With or without Mum's help, I had to stop him.

But I would need back-up. I felt inside my pocket for the piece of paper I'd taken and gripped it tight in my fist.

Upstairs in my room, I listened to Dad cleaning his teeth, shutting his bedroom door and climbing into bed. While I waited, I flicked through the book I'd taken from the basement. The writing was small and lots of the words were long and unfamiliar. I could barely read it. After a while, I just scanned the pages, but I couldn't find any mention of the Lacuna Gem. Soon, my eyes blurred with tiredness. Setting the book aside, I waited until I heard snoring, and then opened my door and sneaked downstairs. In my hand, I held the sheet of paper I'd taken from the basement.

Once I was in the hallway, I sat by the phone and clicked on the lamp. For the hundredth time, I wished I had a mobile like every other kid my age but Mum's words rang in my head: *Phones and training don't mix.* Apparently, I wouldn't be able to focus if I could message my friends whenever I wanted. I sighed. 'Friends' was the wrong word. I only had one friend – April. My stomach clenched at the thought of her. I was pretty sure she didn't like me much right now. For the first time in a long time I wished there was someone else I could turn to. But I didn't have any other friends. I thought back to when I first became so unpopular. Year 1 – that was the year. I'd been a troublemaker with my terrible rages and love of throwing chairs. I remembered Mum arguing with parents at the school gates, after they had told their children to stay away from me. Apparently Grandma Elsie hadn't cared that I was a rulebreaker. April was the only person who ever invited me to her birthday parties.

The creak of Dad's bed snapped me out of my thoughts.

I waited with bated breath, listening in case he left his bedroom. Silence.

Keeping my breathing quiet, I pushed all thoughts of school out of my mind. I looked down at the paper in my hands. At the top, in tiny writing, was a phone number.

I rang it.

An electronic voice answered. "Speak passcode."

Passcode?

I turned the paper over and saw a five-digit number in Mum's handwriting. "Eight, seven, two, nine, seven," I said.

After a few moments, the line clicked and a human voice spoke. "Hunters Corp. What's your business?"

"Hello," I said, my voice croaky. "My name's Etty Steele. I'm phoning about my mum. I think—"

"I'm reconnecting you," the voice said.

The line cut off and then another voice spoke – male and gruff. "Hunters Corp," he said. "How can I help you?"

"My name's Etty Steele—"

"Steele?" the man interrupted. "You must be Felicity's daughter."

"Yes. What's happened to my mum?"

"I'm afraid that's classified," the man replied. "Miss Steele, I realise this must be a hard time for you but the company is doing everything in its power to find your mother, I promise you."

"Well, where did she go?"

"Unfortunately, she was taken before she could tell us her location," he replied. "Your mother did things her own way. Take it as a lesson for when you become a hunter. Always follow company rules. Never go out on a mission alone."

"There must be something I can do!" I said.

"You need to be patient and wait for us to do our job."

"Do you know who took her?" I asked.

"I cannot share that information with you, Miss Steele. I must ask that you let the company deal with—"

"Then, I need back-up," I said. "I have to capture a vampire."

The man spluttered. "What?"

"Vladimir Nox," I said. "He's a boy at my school, but he's a vampire. I think—"

"How do you know that name?" the man interrupted.

"I know more than his name. I know where he is."

"Miss Steele," he said, "we have not confirmed if he is a vampire or not yet. Your mother didn't believe he was."

"But he's real. He goes to Brightwood School," I said firmly.

"Miss Steele. Your mother is missing and you're confused. It's natural to be emotional. But you need to stay out of this. It is not a job for little girls."

I clenched my fists. "Well, I'm going to capture him tomorrow, so you'd better be ready to come and get him when I call."

I slammed the phone down and scrunched the paper in my hand.

I'm not just a little girl, I thought angrily. *I'm a hunter.*

CHAPTER 16

THE WORLD FELT out of balance and just plain wrong without Mum. I didn't sleep very well that night. I kept having nightmares in which I was searching for her, and all I could hear was her yelling for help.

I don't think Dad slept well either. The times I woke up, I heard him pacing about in his room. I imagined him staring at his phone, waiting for a call. Occasionally, I'd hear him crying quietly. I think my nightmares were better than listening to that.

As I got ready for school, I tied my hair into a ponytail and glanced in the mirror. I was pale, and there were bags under my eyes.

Clenching my fists, I turned away from the mirror. I packed an extra bag full of my black training clothes. I would need them later. Dad was working so he couldn't pick me up from school. I told him I was going to April's. But if I managed to get the truth out of Dimi, I'd be going to rescue Bane instead. Even if I had to search the whole town, I was determined to find him. I had to do something right.

I have to do something.

The thought of sitting around, waiting to hear what had happened to Mum, was unbearable.

I shoved the magical book into my bag along with Hunters Corp's phone number and then headed for the door. Halfway there, I stopped. I walked over to my sock drawer. As I reached inside it, I paused. I almost turned away, but then I dug through all the socks until I reached the bottom.

There it was, hidden from sight. My ironwood stake. I'd chosen ironwood because it was hard to break and it didn't splinter easily. It would be perfect for stabbing a vampire.

I grabbed it and shoved it down the waistband of my trousers, covering it with my school jumper. I just hoped I wouldn't have to use it.

"Maybe I should call the police," Dad said as he drove me to school. It was a grey, cloudy day with spots of rain hitting the windows.

"You can't," I replied. "The police can't get involved in vampire stuff. They wouldn't believe you."

"I should be doing something," he whispered, his voice wobbly.

"Hunters Corp would cut us off completely if you got the police involved. They might even stop searching for Mum."

"I know," he said. "Your mum would say the same thing. I'm just worried about her."

I squeezed his hand. "Me too."

"Don't go anywhere with April after school," he said. "Stay at her house. I don't want you out in the dark." He looked miserable. "I can't lose you as well."

"We'll go straight to hers," I lied, feeling awful.

"Is April's gran picking you up?" he asked.

"Yes," I said. Another lie. No one was picking me up.

He kissed me goodbye and I marched into school, clutching my bag of hunter clothes. I pulled my hood up against the rain as I scanned the playground.

The police were still searching for Bane. One of their cars was flashing blue and red lights in the car park.

They should have been after Dimi. He was the last person Bane had seen before he disappeared.

My stomach churned.

Something just didn't fit, though. I thought of the witches' prophecy. Why was Dimi pretending he was a normal schoolkid if he was so powerful? Did he need children for something? Was that why he was hanging around in a school?

After a few minutes, I went to hide in the trees on the school field. I had a plan to get Dimi alone, but I had to be late for school for it to work. It was cold waiting outside but at least the trees protected me from the rain.

Once the playground was empty and the school was quiet, I walked into the office. I was five minutes late. They asked me to sign in and then I made my way to class, my shoes wet and squelchy.

"Miss Gravel," I said as I walked into class, "the office needs to speak to Dimi and me."

I crossed my fingers behind my back, hoping she would believe my lie.

Her brow furrowed, making her glasses go wonky, but she nodded.

Dimi rose from his seat and slowly made his way

towards me. His sunglasses and bowtie were purple. He appeared so harmless, it was almost impossible to believe he was a vampire.

He followed me out of class. He didn't walk beside me. Instead, he hung back a few steps. Neither of us spoke.

Nearly there, I thought.

Moving like lightning, I grabbed his arm and pulled him into the girls' toilets and shut the door behind us.

Dimi backed away towards the opposite wall, which had the hand-dryer on it. Mirrors and sinks lined one wall, and toilet cubicles the other.

"Wh-what do you want?" he asked, his voice shaking.

"I know what you are," I said.

"I don't know what you're talking about," he replied, taking another step back. He bumped into the hand-dryer and set it off. The noise made him jump. He breathed heavily, his hand over his heart.

This is all an act, I told myself. *He's not really afraid.*

"You're a vampire," I said.

I didn't think it was possible for his face to go any paler. But it did.

"N-no," he said.

"Your skin is pale, you wear sunglasses indoors, you're icy cold and you drink human blood."

He sank to his knees and buried his head in his hands.

I scowled. "What did you do to Bane Larkin?"

His sunglasses slipped down to reveal wide, panic-stricken eyes. His pupils were huge. "Bane?" he said. "N-nothing. I didn't do anything to him."

"Did you drink his blood?"

"No!"

"You were the last person to see him," I said. "He annoyed you, so you hurt him."

Dimi's shoulders slumped. "How d-did you know?" he asked.

A thrill of triumph rushed through me. "Vampires are evil killers," I replied. "I knew it had to be you."

He shook his head. "I didn't hurt anyone, I swear! I meant, how did you know I was a vampire?"

"What?" I said, taken aback.

"I am a vampire." He stumbled to his feet and pushed his purple sunglasses back into place. "But I d-didn't hurt anyone. I'm n-not evil."

"Of course you are! You drink human blood!"

"No," he replied. "I've never had a drop of blood. Not even animal blood. I can't..." His voice trailed off.

I narrowed my eyes in suspicion. "Then what were you drinking yesterday?"

"Cranberry juice," he replied, "just like I said."

"Vampires can't survive without blood."

"I can," he said. "I don't need blood. I eat normal food."

"You're lying," I said. "Vampires can't survive without blood. You did something to Bane Larkin. You must have done."

"I didn't!"

"Then what happened to him?" I asked. "He was teasing you and then you walked off together. What happened after that?"

Dimi's hands shook. "We w-walked down the stairs and then he pushed me against the wall. He said I was a f-fairy and then he stole my sunglasses and put them on."

"So, what did you do?" I asked. "Did you get angry? Did you attack him?"

"N-no!" he said. "I didn't do anything. I g-got out my spare sunglasses. He walked off, wearing my p-purple ones."

"Then what?"

"Nothing," he said. "I went d-downstairs, bumped into April."

This can't be true, I thought. *It's all lies. Vampires have to drink blood to survive – that's what Mum has always told me. And if Dimi didn't make Bane Larkin vanish, then who did?*

"What about the vampire clan?" I asked. "What do you know about them? They've killed two women."

"I-I don't know anything about a clan," he said and then his voice cracked. "Killed? People have been killed?"

"Yes," I replied. "The clan is looking for a gem. Do you know anything about that?"

"No."

"I don't believe you," I said. "I don't believe anything you've told me."

I pulled the stake out of my waistband. Dimi backed up against the wall, holding up his hands in surrender.

"Please," he said, "I'm telling the truth."

"I'm capturing you and sending you to Traxis," I told him.

"N-no, not there!"

He glanced around for an exit, but there was no escape. I was blocking the only way out.

"On the way to hunter headquarters, you're going to tell me where Bane Larkin is."

As I got closer to him, he started to cry quietly.

"I'm telling the truth," he said. "I don't know anything

about a clan or what happened to Bane. I just walked downstairs and met April. I didn't hurt Bane."

A tear slid down his cheek.

"You're lying," I retorted, "and you have no way to prove your story."

I was about to reach out and grab him when the door to the toilets burst open. I spun around and dropped the stake. April stood in the doorway. She walked in, her arms crossed over her chest.

"Actually, he can," she said in a loud, but shaky voice. "He can prove he's telling the truth. He can prove it because I was there and I know where Bane went."

CHAPTER 17

I STARED AT April in shock.

"You heard all that?" I asked.

"I needed the toilet," she replied, "but then I heard you talking so I listened outside the door."

I picked up my stake and gripped it tightly. "Be careful," I told her. "He's dangerous."

"So, Dimi's a vampire?" she asked.

I nodded.

"If that's true," she said, "then you must be a vampire hunter."

My mouth fell open. How did she know about vampire hunters?

"My grandma told me," April said, and held up her hand to show me her ring. "When she told me about witches, she also told me about vampires and hunters and fairies and a lot of other things too. So if Dimi really is a vampire and you're a hunter, then it must be true. I'm a witch." As she said the last word, she squirmed.

"Yes," I replied.

"Did you know the whole time?" she asked me. "Did you know witches were real?"

"Not at first," I said, wanting to melt into the floor and vanish, "but then… I found out."

She cast her eyes down. "You should've told me."

"I tried, but—"

"It makes sense now," she interrupted, facing Dimi. "The sunglasses, the way Etty didn't want to be near you. And you're so pale." She stepped towards him.

"Stay back, April," I warned her. "Did your grandma tell you what vampires do to humans?"

April's shoulders stiffened. "She said they drink human blood."

"I have to take him to Traxis," I said.

Dimi came to stand next to me, his head down. "I can't fight you," he said, "so let's just go."

"Dimi," April said, "you're not going anywhere. You didn't do anything wrong." She threw me a determined look. "I can tell you what really happened yesterday."

Part of me thought I should just ignore her and take Dimi away – but what if she was right? Could Dimi be innocent?

He can't be! I thought. *The vampire in the graveyard said Dimi was going to be the strongest, cruellest vampire in the world.*

April went to stand in front of the door. "I'm not letting you take him until you've listened to me," she said firmly.

"Fine," I replied. "What happened?"

"Well," she said, "on the way to lunch I saw Bane Larkin walking downstairs. He was wearing Dimi's sunglasses and I knew Dimi wouldn't have given them to him. So I walked up to Bane to tell him to give them back. Like I expected, he just laughed at me and said he was going outside."

"And then what?" I asked impatiently.

"He walked out the main doors and onto the field," she replied. "After that, Dimi came downstairs. He was upset, so we went to an empty classroom to eat lunch together."

"What about Bane?" I asked.

"I didn't see him again," she said, "but I was with Dimi the whole lunchtime. He couldn't have done anything to Bane. He was with me."

I rubbed my forehead.

What was I going to do? Bane had vanished. Mum had vanished. And if Dimi wasn't responsible, who was? And how would I find them?

"Fine," I said to Dimi. "Maybe you didn't have anything to do with what happened to Bane, but you have to tell me about the new vampire clan in town."

"I d-don't know anything about a clan," he said.

I let out a frustrated groan.

"There's a clan in town?" April asked, grimacing.

"They're monsters," I said, thinking of what they'd done to Helen and Deidre. "I need to know where they are."

"I'm s-sorry," Dimi muttered. "I don't know anything."

A vein throbbed in my neck, threatening to burst. How could he know nothing? He was a vampire!

My mouth opened. I wasn't sure whether I was going to moan in defeat or scream in anger. Before I made a sound, however, April spoke up. "Maybe it was the vampire clan," she said. "Maybe they're the ones who took Bane."

Her words made me falter. The clan?

It could've been them, I thought. But why would they

steal a gem and then kidnap a boy from school? They wouldn't. They'd have no interest in a schoolkid. But the clan might have taken someone else, someone who was searching for them.

Mum!

The clan had taken Mum! How had I not seen it before?

"What is it?" April asked.

I was about to tell them about Mum's disappearance, but I stopped myself: I couldn't trust Dimi with something like this, and April would worry if she found out.

"I'm just thinking about Bane," I said. "We need to find him."

Dimi took his sunglasses off and squinted in the light. His jaw was tight, as if the brightness caused him pain.

"I think I might be able to help you find Bane," he said in his soft voice.

"How?" I asked sharply.

"I have strong senses," he replied. "If we f-find where Bane disappeared, I might be able to track his scent."

April smiled encouragingly. "We're going to find him," she said.

I didn't say anything. There was no way Bane had been taken by the vampire clan. His disappearance had something to do with Dimi – I was sure of it.

"Etty?" April asked, snapping me out of my thoughts. "What do you think?"

"It's worth a try."

I gazed at Dimi. *I'll be keeping my eye on you,* I thought.

CHAPTER 18

WHEN THE BELL rang for break, the three of us made our way outside. The plan was to sneak onto the field and use Dimi's vampire senses to track Bane.

It was still raining so I pulled the hood of my black leather jacket up over my head. April's yellow coat was fluffy and not very waterproof. With the hood up, she looked like a yellow teddy bear, but she swore it was the warmest thing in the world. Dimi, on the other hand, didn't have a hood. His long black coat just had a high collar. He reminded me of the vampires I'd seen in films – he was like a miniature Dracula.

As we sneaked past the teachers and onto the field (which was off-limits when it rained), I worried that this was a very bad idea. We would be alone: just April, me and a bloodsucking vampire.

When we were out of sight of any adults, Dimi stopped and drew in a deep breath through his nose.

"Well?" I asked, on edge. "Can you smell anything?"

He shook his head. "Sorry," he replied, "I just need a moment to c-concentrate."

April was on the lookout in case any teachers saw us. I was busy keeping an eye on Dimi.

Abruptly, he went completely still. He stepped forward. Then again. And again. He was leading us away from school towards the trees at the edge of the field. I glanced back. April was following us.

Finally, Dimi stopped. I held my breath. We were on the other side of the field, the trees and bushes in front of us dark and swaying in the wind. Anything could have been hiding in there.

He sniffed at the air then pulled a disgusted face. "This is where Bane was taken," he said, "but his scent has completely disappeared."

Disappeared? "What do you mean?"

"I think the person who t-took him had a much stronger smell," he answered. "It's horrible."

April caught up with us, and she sniffed the air as well. "I can't smell anything."

"I can only smell it b-because I'm using my vampire senses," Dimi told her. "Etty can probably smell it too if she's a hunter."

My cheeks burned hot. "I don't have my hunter senses yet," I said irritably.

"Oh," Dimi replied, bowing his head.

There was a long silence.

"So, what's the smell?" April asked.

"Cabbage," Dimi said. "The person who took Bane stank of cabbage."

As soon as he said it, my heart skipped a beat. My mind flashed back to the graveyard and the ratty vampire. I remembered the rash on his skin and his dirty clothes, but most of all I remembered his smell. He'd reeked of cabbage.

Raif had taken Bane.

My heart dropped like a stone. An image of Mum about to stab Raif through the heart swam in my mind. I'd stopped her. I'd let Raif go.

This is my fault…

"I know who took him," I said, silently cursing myself. "And I know where to go."

"So," April said, "that means Dimi was telling the truth. He didn't do anything to Bane."

That doesn't mean he's good, I thought.

"Maybe not all vampires are evil," April said. "Dimi's nothing like the vampires in films and stories. All they care about is blood and killing things."

"But that *is* all vampires care about," I replied.

"Well, not Dimi," she said.

"According to *him*," I murmured irritably.

April looked at Dimi apologetically. "Well, maybe there's stuff we don't know about real vampires. I mean, I always thought they burned in sunlight and didn't have a heartbeat."

"That's just superstitious rubbish," I told her. "Vampires can go in the sun but it hurts their eyes. They're alive, but pale. They like graveyards. They don't have emotions, and they only care about blood. That sums them up pretty well."

April folded her arms, clearly unimpressed.

I knew what she was thinking – that I was being unkind, unfair. She thought I should've been nicer to Dimi, but she didn't know vampires like I did. Mum had been preparing me to deal with them since I learned to walk. What I'd said was true – vampires were emotionless, bloodsucking monsters.

Dimi was fiddling nervously with the sleeves of his coat. I wondered if he would say anything. "Most of us are evil," he said, "but I promise you I'm not."

"Why?" I asked, my voice stiff. "What makes you so different?"

"I-I'm not allowed to tell you," he replied.

"Is it something to do with you being born a vampire, and not bitten?"

He froze. "What?" he said. "H-how do you know that? No one is supposed to know that."

"Is that why you can eat normal food?" I asked.

"Y-yes," he said, clearly shaken. "Born vampires can choose whether they eat food or blood. But if they choose blood…" He pulled a sour face.

"What happens?"

"They turn evil."

"So," April said, "that's why you're good. You've never drunk blood."

He nodded.

"What about your dad?" I asked. "Is he a vampire? Does he drink blood?"

"Y-yes, he's a born vampire too and, no, he doesn't drink blood. He eats food like me."

"That can't be true," I cut in. "If it was possible for vampires to be good, my mum would have told me. She said all vampires are evil and they all drink blood. Every single one."

"I'm not evil and neither's my dad," Dimi said, "and I can prove it." He folded his arms. "But I'll need some blood."

"Blood?" I said. "No way! Do you think we're mad?"

"It's the only way to prove it," he said. "I-I'm not going to hurt anyone, I promise."

April tugged something off one of the bushes and brought it over to Dimi. It was a thorn.

"What are you doing?" I asked.

April pricked her finger and a bead of blood popped up. I rushed towards her but she glared at me. "Wait!" she said.

Against all my instincts, I stopped.

With every nerve on end, I watched as Dimi moved his hand towards the blood on her finger. I thought he was going to touch it but, as the tips of his fingers got close, the bead of blood began to move away from him. It crawled backwards along April's finger. I leaned closer.

I must be seeing things, I thought.

He moved his hand again and the bead moved further away as if it was repelled by him.

I don't believe it.

Next, he held his hands cupped together. "Try to drop the blood into my palms," he said to April. Her face had gone pale. Without speaking, she lifted her finger so it was above Dimi's hands and she let the drop of blood fall. It should've landed in his palms but at the last moment, the crimson bead drifted sideways as if it had been caught by an imaginary wind. It missed his hand. The blood landed on the grass.

I was stunned.

April blinked. And again. "How?" she said.

"I-I don't know," Dimi replied. "Ever since I can remember, blood hasn't been able to touch me or even come near me. The only blood I can touch is my own."

"Are all vampires like you?" April asked.

"I don't think so," he said. "I think I'm the only one."

So Mum was wrong. A vampire *could* live without blood. If that was true, then was Dimi a good vampire?

No, I thought. *The witches' prophecy said he would be cruel and powerful.*

"You're one of a kind," April said to Dimi. She reached out to take his hand. When their hands touched, she gasped.

"Sorry," she said. "I'm still getting used to how cold you are."

"That's okay," he replied. "It's nice to have someone t-touch me. People don't usually do that."

"Well," she said, "I'm a witch and Etty's a vampire hunter, so you're not *that* different."

Dimi's cheeks turned pink.

April took my hand so the three of us were linked. I wanted to pull away.

I wished I could see Dimi's eyes behind his sunglasses. What was he thinking? What was he planning?

Finally, April released our hands. "Are you going to tell us, then?" she asked me.

"What?"

"Who took Bane!" she said. "And where do we have to go?"

"His name's Raif," I told her. "He's a vampire, and we have to go to the place vampires love most."

"Where?" they asked.

"The graveyard."

CHAPTER 19

AT THE END of break, I went to my peg and took out the magic book from my bag. If the vampire clan had taken Mum, I needed to find out why they were here in Brightwood. That meant learning more about the gem they'd stolen. When I gave the book to April, she held it gingerly.

"It's about magic," I told her as we stood outside class. "I need you to look for something in there. It's called the Lacuna Gem. I've already tried, but… books aren't my thing."

"So that's why you were asking me about gems yesterday," she said.

I winced as I remembered how I'd lied to her.

"I can't believe you knew about witches and you didn't tell me," she said, her voice quivering. "I thought I was going mad. I thought Grandma was insane."

"I know. I—"

"Is there an index?" she asked as she turned to the back of the book.

"I don't think so," I muttered, my stomach churning.

"I'll have a look during maths," she told me and then she walked into class without saying goodbye.

At lunchtime, Bane Larkin was still missing and the police were hanging around outside. I felt restless. I wanted school to finish already. I wanted to go to the graveyard. Every moment we were stuck here, the more chance there was that something terrible would happen to Bane or Mum.

April, Dimi and I found an empty classroom to eat our lunch. Today, his drink bottle was filled with orange juice. I wished April and I could sit alone. I wanted to apologise to her. I'd known she was a witch and I'd had every chance to tell her, but, like a coward, I hadn't. If April had kept a secret like that from me, I would've been mad too.

She pulled the magic book out of her bag.

"Why am I trying to find a gem?" she asked. "I haven't found any mention of Lacuna and I spent half of maths looking."

"You remember the vampire clan I told you about?" I said.

April and Dimi nodded.

"Well, they took the Lacuna Gem from…" I met April's eyes and my voice died in my throat. Could I really tell her where the gem had come from? That Helen had been murdered for it? Deidre too? But the thought of not telling her seemed worse, much worse.

April frowned. "Who'd they take it from?"

"There's something I need to tell you," I said. "It's about Helen." I fiddled with the catch on my lunchbox. "I know how she really died."

April turned white.

I had to force the words out of my mouth, dreading her reaction. "She... she was poisoned."

April's hand flew to her mouth. "Someone poisoned her?" she said, her voice high-pitched. "Who?"

"It was the vampire clan," I told her. "They were trying to find the Lacuna Gem. Helen was a witch. They thought she was guarding it."

April cast her eyes down and the magic book slipped from her fingers. I went over to comfort her but she stood up and wiped her eyes. "I'm fine," she said.

"Are you sure?" I asked.

"Did Helen have the gem?" April asked.

"No," I replied quietly. I told them about Deidre Salamay – how she had kept the gem in her cellar and the vampires had poisoned her so they could take the gem.

"Two women killed," April said, falling back into her seat, "all for a shiny bit of stone."

I crouched beside her, wishing I could find the words to comfort her, but she smiled weakly and turned her attention back to the magic book. Feeling lousy, I returned to my seat. While April flicked through the book, I picked at my lunch. With her attention focused on the worn pages, Dimi and I were left in silence. He kept opening his mouth as if he was going to say something to me, but then he took another bite of food instead. I was glad. I didn't want to speak to him.

"Ah!" April said with fierce triumph. "I found it!"

I jerked forward in my seat.

She moved her lunchbox out of the way and spread the book open in the middle of the table. In the bottom left-hand corner of the page was a picture of a square black gem set into a thick silver bracelet that looked more like a shackle than a piece of jewellery. Next to the picture were the words *Lacuna Gem.*

"It says that the gem has the power to undo magic," April told us. "So if someone wears the bracelet, magic doesn't work on them."

"Vampires are afraid of witches," Dimi said. "Maybe the leader of the clan wants to be immune to magic so he can fight a witch."

April took the book back and tucked it into her bag. "What about Bane?" she said. "He must be linked to the gem somehow. That's why the clan took him as well."

"Raif took Bane, not the clan," I reminded her.

"Maybe he's working for them," she said.

I resisted the urge to scoff. "You wouldn't be saying that if you'd met Raif," I said. I couldn't imagine a powerful vampire clan using someone like Raif to do their dirty work. Yet hadn't he told Mum he came to Brightwood to join the clan? Maybe he'd kidnapped Bane to impress them.

"But why?" I said. "Why would a vampire clan want Bane – a normal schoolboy – and a gem that blocks magic? What's their plan?"

"Maybe Bane's a witch," Dimi said.

"Or maybe he's a three-headed alien," I replied nastily.

April kicked me under the table.

"Sorry," I mumbled.

"I guess we don't have any answers," April said.

She was right. Bane had gone missing and a clan had stolen a gem – and we had no idea why.

At the end of the day, Mrs Brooks, the head teacher, called a whole-school assembly. She told us to be extra-careful leaving school. Bane still hadn't been found.

I was sitting with April and Dimi on the floor of the hall, which was still sticky from lunch.

"My dad thinks I'm going home with you," I whispered to April. "He's not coming to pick me up, which means I can go to the graveyard."

"Okay," she said. "When my grandma comes, I'll tell her I'm going home with you. That way, I can come to the graveyard as well."

I took her hand. "April," I said, "I don't think you should come with us."

Her eyes met mine and I swore I saw something flash in her pupils, like a strike of lightning or a flicker of fire. "Etty, I'm coming with you," she told me firmly, "and there's nothing you can do about it."

"But—"

"I'm coming," she said. Her eyes dared me to argue with her.

I stared at her for a moment and then nodded. "Fine."

"What about you, Dimi?" April asked him.

"I'll sneak out of school without telling my dad," he said to her. "He'd never let me go otherwise. Ever since our house got broken into, he hardly lets me out of his sight."

"Is it a good idea to trick him like that?" April asked.

"Dimi, your dad's a vampire," I reminded him. "I don't think we should make him angry."

"I know," he said, "but I c-can't leave you two to do this on your own. What if something happens to you?"

I'm more worried about you coming with us, I thought. "Will your dad be able to track us?" I asked.

"Yes, but I'll distract him."

"How?" April and I asked.

"I'll fly around town for a bit to make my scent hard to trace."

"Fly?" April exclaimed.

I shut my eyes and cursed myself for not thinking of it before. Dimi was a born vampire! "You can turn into a bat, can't you?" I said.

"Yes. I'm not very good at it, though."

Before we could say anything else, Mrs Brooks ended the assembly and Miss Gravel led our class upstairs to get our things.

Once we were in the cloakroom, I told Dimi to meet us outside school and then I changed into my black hunter clothes, leaving my school stuff on my peg. Hoping I wouldn't have to use it, I slipped the stake into the long pocket at the front of my hoodie. Meanwhile, April watched in silence.

When I was ready, we were the only ones left in the cloak-room. Miss Gravel had walked everyone else downstairs.

April twisted her ring around on her finger.

"I still can't believe all this is real," she said gloomily. "I'm a witch and you're a vampire hunter..."

"I'm sorry I didn't tell you," I replied, wincing. "I wanted to. But it's against the rules for humans to know about us."

She didn't say anything.

"April," I said, my voice breaking slightly.

"I know," she finally replied. "I know why you couldn't say anything – your mum can be a little scary."

I nodded.

"At least Gran isn't insane," she said. "And now I know

why you were being so mean to Dimi. But, Etty, I think you need to give him a chance."

"He's a vampire," I retorted. "And I know things about him, things that prove he's not as good and kind as he pretends he is."

"Well, whatever you've found out, it must be wrong," she said.

"Don't you want to know?"

"No," she answered simply. "Dimi can't touch blood. He gets nervous around people he doesn't know. Come on, Etty! He loves his eighty-year-old tutor! He's not evil. I don't care that he's a vampire."

"There's no such thing as a good vampire, April," I told her.

Her eyebrows drew together in worry but she didn't argue.

As we made our way back downstairs she glanced at my black hoodie and leggings. "You look older in those," she said.

"They're easier to fight in."

"Will there be fighting?" she asked.

"Not for you," I replied.

She fell silent.

We told Miss Gravel that April's grandma was taking me home and I sighed in relief when she let us leave together. April frowned as we walked out of the school gates.

Maybe I shouldn't bring her with me, I thought. *She could get hurt.*

Then, I tried to imagine leaving April behind.

She'd kill me.

Her grandma's Beetle was a car that actually looked like a bug. Its headlights were like fat, bulbous eyes.

She peered out of the window at us and smiled. All I could think about were the ice handcuffs she'd magicked around my wrists and ankles. Grandma Elsie wasn't the harmless old lady I'd thought she was. She'd taken me down in a moment with just a wave of her hand.

"I'm going home with Etty," April told her, averting her eyes. She wasn't the best liar.

The old woman sent her grand-daughter a long, piercing stare. "Of course you are," she said kindly – but the way she said it made me think she didn't believe April one bit.

"See you later, then," April said.

Grandma Elsie gripped her wrist, then took off one of her necklaces. It had a circular crystal hanging from it. At first, I was sure the crystal was blue, but as the gold chain of the necklace left Elsie's neck, its colour faded and it turned clear. Reaching out of the window, Elsie put the chain around April's neck. I blinked as the crystal changed colour again. It was now yellow. In fact, it was the exact same shade as April's ring…

"But it was blue…" April said in bewilderment.

"Its colour comes from the witch wearing it," Grandma Elsie replied. "For me, it was blue. For you, it is yellow."

"I can't take this," April said. "It's your favourite."

"Yes, it's my lucky charm," Grandma Elsie replied, "but I think it's time I passed it on to you." She pressed her wrinkled finger to the crystal. "It is a protection charm. A powerful one."

April and I glanced at each other.

Before April could say any more, her grandma drove off, a cloud of black smoke pluming from the exhaust of her rickety car.

Wondering what Grandma Elsie had meant, I walked with April to the end of the road where we found Dimi waiting for us, his coat wrapped around him and his hands deep in his pockets. He was shivering even though it wasn't that cold.

The rain had soaked his black hair.

"You're frozen," April said when we caught up to him.

"I-I'm okay," he replied, his lips trembling. "I just got cold flying around. Bats don't wear c-clothes."

"Here," she said, "my coat's much warmer than yours."

I thought he was going to refuse, but he took one look at the fluffy coat with its fleece lining and quickly swapped with her.

The Dracula coat suited April surprisingly well. Dimi looked like an undead canary.

"I never thought I'd see a vampire in a fluffy yellow coat," I commented.

Dimi grinned and stroked the fur.

"I think I like it b-better than my own coat," he said, admiring himself. "I might get one in purple."

"It suits you," April said. "What do you think, Etty?"

I rolled my eyes. "I think we need to leave."

They nodded a little apprehensively. We set off towards the graveyard.

CHAPTER 20

IT WAS A short bus ride to the graveyard. An old woman sent us a kind smile as we sat down on the bus, and April waved politely to her. Dimi didn't seem to notice. He sat by the window, stroking his coat. April was beside him and I sat opposite.

Dimi was quiet. I wondered if he was thinking about his dad (who was probably out searching for him at this very moment). I wondered how angry he'd be if he found us. After all, Dimi had flown around town as a bat just so his dad couldn't track us. I tried to imagine Dimi transforming. Did vampires just vanish in a puff of smoke and then reappear as a bat, or was there a flash?

"How did you learn?" I asked Dimi. "I mean, how did you learn to change into a bat?"

"M-my dad taught me," he said, his voice wary. "He wanted me to be able to escape if something bad happened. But I g-get nervous. I can't do it when I'm nervous."

"What else can vampires do?" I asked.

"Th-there are five powers," he said. "Healing, t-turning

into a bat, glamouring, controlling people's emotions..."
His voice trailed off. "Th-there's one more, but Dad won't
tell me that one."

"What's glamouring?" April and I asked.

"We can change." He paused as if he wasn't sure how to
explain it. "We can glamour ourselves so we look more...
friendly and beautiful."

"That seems like a strange power," April said.

"I don't know why vampires need so many powers,"
Dimi replied.

I do, I thought. *If you can make yourself look friendly
and beautiful, you can get innocent humans to trust you. And
then... you can bite them.*

I sat forward in my seat, anxious to arrive at the graveyard.

"So," April said worriedly, "we're going to a graveyard to
talk to a vampire. This is a bad idea, isn't it?"

"It's dangerous," I told her. "That's why you and Dimi
are waiting outside."

"No way!" April said. "Helen was poisoned by vampires.
You're not leaving me behind."

I folded my arms. "But I'm a vampire hunter. I can look
after myself. You're—"

"A witch," she interrupted. "And, anyway, I can look
after myself too."

"April, we don't even know if you have any powers. I've
been training for years to fight vampires."

Something seemed to click in her brain. "Your mum
isn't really a kickboxing champion, is she?"

"Nope. She's a vampire hunter, and she's been training
me since I was three."

"No wonder you kept beating everyone up when we were little," she said.

After that, she didn't speak. I hoped she'd decided to let me go into the graveyard alone, but something told me that was the exact opposite of what she was going to do.

We jolted in our seats when the bus stopped outside St Luke's Church.

When we finally stood at the gate to the graveyard, my stomach twisted itself into knots. The rain spat in our faces. The wind howled eerily. As I pushed open the gate, its rusty hinges creaked.

I opened my mouth to speak but April cut me off. "Before you say anything, I'm coming with you and that's that."

"Me too," Dimi agreed.

"Fine," I said to April, then turned to Dimi. "Not you," I said firmly. "You'll stay here."

"Wh-what?" he asked.

"Etty," April said, "you can't be serious. You still don't trust him?"

"Vampires gain power in graveyards," I said. "He can wait here until we return."

Without looking back, I strode into the graveyard. For a moment, I thought April was going to stay with Dimi, but then I heard her light steps behind me.

"What's wrong?" she asked once she'd caught up.

That wasn't what I'd expected her to say at all. I'd been half expecting her to shout at me. Not knowing how to reply, I didn't answer. Instead, I kept my eyes alert for vampires, especially a ratty one with bad skin.

"Etty," she continued in her soft voice. "Your mum's a hunter. Why isn't she here?"

I stopped.

"Why are we doing this alone?" she asked. Her voice was even softer than before. "If this is her job, your mum should be helping us."

My throat went tight. "I…" I wanted to tell her, but I couldn't make the words come out.

"Something's happened to her, hasn't it?" April said.

I drew in a deep, shaky breath and nodded.

She took my hand and tried to hug me but I pulled back.

"April," I said. "I know you don't want to hear this, but I think… I think Dimi has something to do with all this." I pulled my hand out of her grasp and leaned on a nearby gravestone for support. "The witches have made a prophecy about Dimi. It says he will be the most evil and powerful vampire in the world."

"Dimi?" she said, her tone incredulous. "You don't believe that, do you?"

I shrugged. "I don't know what I believe. If my mum was here, she probably would've killed Dimi as soon as she knew what he was."

"No, she wouldn't," April said, "because Dimi's a good person."

"He's evil," I said. "He's got to be."

"But what if he isn't?" she said simply.

My face twisted into a scowl. Before I could answer, an awful smell filled my nostrils and my blood turned to fire.

The air stank of cabbage.

I whirled around. Raif plodded towards us. His clothes were brown and grey, baggy and ripped. He sniffed his fingers.

"How beautiful!" the ratty vampire squealed, gazing hungrily at April.

My rage boiled over. I darted towards him like a mad-woman. Flying through the air, I landed a kick to his stomach, then lost my balance and fell. Without stopping, I rolled back to my feet. The vampire was doubled over in pain, drawing in deep breaths. When he looked up, his expression was full of shock.

He rushed towards me. He swiped at my shoulder. I dodged the attack and then avoided three more blows. He was fast. His movements were a blur.

Hot rage pulsed through me. I barrelled into him. He fell back and slammed into the dirt with a groan. Before he could move, I pinned him down roughly.

"Was it you?" I growled. "Did you take that boy from school? Did you do something to my mum?"

Raif's eyes widened. "I will tell you," he said, "but only if you promise to let me go."

I pressed him harder against the ground.

Let him go?

My hand inched towards the stake in my hoodie. I could end this now – but if I did, I would never find out what had happened to Bane.

"Fine," I replied through gritted teeth. "Now tell me what you know. Did you take that boy?"

The vampire nodded. "Yes," he said. "I took the boy from school – snatched him up when no one was looking."

My heart plummeted. Mum had warned me he would hurt someone, and she was right! I'd helped him escape and he'd gone and kidnapped Bane.

"Why did you do it?" I yelled.

Raif didn't respond at first. He glanced about as if he was

afraid someone might be listening. "I took him to the clan," he said. "Their leader wanted to see him."

"Their leader. Who is he?"

"Not 'he'!" Raif said, and a flicker of excitement lit up his scabby features. "The leader is a 'she' – the vampire queen!".

Vampire queen? I'd never heard of a vampire queen before.

"She leads the clan," Raif said. "She bit most of them herself. Beautiful and terrible she is. A true lady! She wanted the boy, so I kidnapped him and took him to her ship. Such a wondrous woman."

"Why does the queen want a schoolkid?" I asked.

"She's going to use the gem on him," he replied. "He is special. He will wear the bracelet and something great will happen! He will be reborn! He'll be the queen's unstoppable assassin!"

Bane? Unstoppable? It didn't make sense. What was so special about Bane? Then, it hit me like a truck. "He's a vampire!" I said.

"Of course he's a vampire!" Raif squealed, shaking with excitement.

I'd been right all along. Somehow Bane had hidden it from Mum all those years ago and now the vampire queen wanted Bane to join her clan.

"You said you took him to a ship," I said. "Where is this ship?"

"It's hidden in the sea cave at Seer's Cove. It's a beautiful place!"

Seer's Cove. It shocked me to think of vampires being there. I remembered running on that small beach as a child. Dad taught me to swim in the shallows of the cove. I remembered Mum grabbing me by the arms and throwing me into the deeper water.

"It's sink or swim," she'd said. She'd held me as I sputtered. I'd kicked my legs and fought to keep my head above water. For a moment, I'd caught a look of something like pride flash across her face.

We'd only gone to the cove in the summer, when Baywater Beach was too busy with tourists. It had been a quiet, restful place. Now it was infested with a clan of vampires.

"You know the place?" Raif asked.

"I went there when I was young," I told him distractedly.

"I bet that wonderful mother of yours took you there," he said. "She doesn't like it much now though, I don't think!" He cackled madly.

"What?" I said, my attention snapping from my thoughts. Terror coursed through me. "My mum's there?"

"Oh yes," he purred. "Your dear, sweet mother found the queen's hideout and they captured her. But don't worry, the queen's going to honour her greatly."

My stomach turned over at that. "What's the queen going to do?"

"She'll drink your mother's blood!" Raif yelled. "It's a great honour! Then she'll throw your kind, loving mother over the side of the ship. Mummy dearest will float out into the ocean, gone forever."

It felt like my heart had stopped beating. The earth was tilting under my feet. "When will it happen?"

"Midnight," he said. "That's when the moon will be fullest. *Midnight…*

"I've told you everything I know," he said. "Now let me go."

I glowered at him, imagining all the evil things he could still do.

"No," I replied finally. "I let you go once before, remember? I stopped my mum killing you. And then what did you do? You kidnapped a schoolkid! I can't release you. I won't."

"That kid is a vampire!" he spat. "I didn't hurt anyone!"

"But the queen's going to turn him into an unstoppable assassin!" I replied. "And that's because I let you go. But not this time."

I reached into my hoodie and pulled out my iron-wood stake.

Raif's eyes flashed with hatred. He twisted free from my grip with a burst of strength that caught me by surprise. He shoved me in the chest. The world spun as I flew through the air. I hit the ground hard. Panting for breath, I clutched my chest. I couldn't breathe. He'd winded me.

Staggering to my feet, I glanced around, the stake in my hand. My eyes widened when I finally saw him. With one arm he held April tightly in front of him, and with his free hand he pressed a knife to her throat. The anger drained out of me. I dropped the stake.

Her name came out of my mouth like a breath. "April."

"You hunters are all the same!" Raif spat. He wasn't grinning any more. "You think you're better than us? You're killers too!"

"Please," I said, holding my hands up in surrender. It was all I could do. I was too far away to act. Raif could cut April's throat before I took a single step toward him.

My hands shook. "Please don't hurt her."

"You are just like your mother," Raif said, pressing the knife closer to April's neck, "but you are weaker."

April whimpered, her eyes wide with terror. Seeing that look on her face made my legs give way. I fell to my knees.

"Please," I repeated.

Raif sniffed in disgust. "You know what happens if that stake goes through my heart? It turns me to dust!"

"I'm sorry."

My breath died in my throat as he pulled April's head back, exposing her neck. Time seemed to slow down. He brought the knife to her skin. April panted. The blade bit into her flesh. A single drop of blood trickled down her neck.

Suddenly, there was a thud. I watched, confused, as Raif's eyes rolled back and the knife slipped out of his hand. Like a sack of potatoes, he collapsed to the ground. He was unconscious!

April wiped her fingers over the shallow cut on her neck. I watched the blood smear her skin. Then I noticed who was standing behind her.

Dimi.

He held a thick tree branch and stared at Raif's unconscious body with wide, shock-filled eyes. He'd hit him from behind. He'd stopped Raif!

"You saved me," April said to Dimi.

He didn't reply. He was still gaping at Raif in stunned silence.

Somehow, I managed to get my shaking legs to work. I stood up and stumbled over to April.

"Are you okay?" I asked.

She nodded, then wrapped her arms around me. I could feel her sobbing. Once she'd stopped crying, she let go of me and wiped away the tears on her cheeks.

"I'm okay," she said. "Dimi saved me."

"I-I knocked him out," Dimi said, his voice full of surprise.

I didn't know what to say. It didn't make any sense. Nothing made sense. Who was this strange boy? He had saved April while I'd watched, completely useless. Why had he done it? If he was really the cruellest vampire that had ever lived, then why had he saved her?

April pulled him into a ferocious hug. I turned away. I didn't want to see. My shoes sank into the mud as I walked over to the stake I'd dropped.

Should I have let Raif go like I promised? Was this my fault? Had I almost got April killed?

Mum's words echoed in my head: *We have to do terrible things. That's what hunters do.*

I didn't want to be a killer.

Then you will never be a hunter.

I remembered the disappointment in my mum's eyes after I'd let Raif escape from her.

I crouched down and reached towards the stake where it lay on the muddy ground. My hand paused.

I could leave it here. I could let it sink into the mud and be forgotten.

"Etty!" April called to me. "We should go! If we want to get to Seer's Cove before it gets dark, we need to leave now!"

The sharp, pointed piece of wood lay there, waiting.

You will never be a hunter.

I clenched my jaw and picked up the stake. It slid easily into the pocket of my hoodie – invisible to everyone but me.

April pulled me to one side on the way back to the road, telling Dimi to carry on ahead. The gravestones watched us grimly and the sky darkened with clouds.

"Are you okay?" she asked.

"I'm fine."

"What happened to Bane wasn't your fault," she said. "Saving Raif was the right thing to do."

"I should've let Mum kill him," I replied. "Then none of this would've happened."

"You're not a killer, Etty."

I kicked a rock. It skittered across the mud and struck a gravestone, leaving a small crack. "I'm a hunter," I said. "I'm supposed to hunt vampires."

April walked over to the cracked gravestone and laid her hand on it. "No, Etty," she said. "You're supposed to protect people." Her fingers traced over the crack and she sighed before turning her back on me and walking off.

You're right, I thought, *and I'm going to protect you, I promise.*

CHAPTER 21

SEER'S COVE WAS a small beach to the south of Brightwood, surrounded by cliffs. As the bus drew nearer, the stake in my pocket seemed to become heavier, as if it was calling out to me.

Apart from us, the bus was empty. No one else was heading to the beach on a day like this. Outside, rain pelted the windows and wind tore at the trees. On one side, cliffs looked out to the churning ocean. On the other, fields stretched towards dark, distant hills. All three of us shivered from the cold – Dimi the worst. His hair was soaked, his lips were blue and his teeth were chattering. April rubbed his arms to try to warm him up.

They sat side by side like that as the bus took us closer to Seer's Cove. The nearer we got, the more afraid I felt.

My mum was on a ship full of vampires. She had been captured and, tonight, the vampire queen was going to drink her blood, then toss her into the ocean.

I willed the bus to go faster. Every muscle in my body was on edge.

As we trundled towards Seer's Cove, April began to fill Dimi in on what Raif had said. When she mentioned the vampire queen, Dimi interrupted her. "Which queen?" he asked.

April faltered.

Seeing her confusion, Dimi said, "Th-there's more than one queen."

I sat bolt upright. "What?"

"D-didn't you know?" he asked.

"No, I didn't," I replied.

Dimi counted on his fingers. "There's a vampire king and queen here in England but also in Russia, America, Canada, Finland, Switzerland, Norway... and I think there's a few more."

My mind whirring, I stood up. My feet began to pace. There were vampire kings and queens in all those countries? Did Mum know about this? Did Hunters Corp know?

"If there's more than one queen," I said, "which one are we on our way to meet?"

"It could be any of them," Dimi said.

I carried on pacing, hardly believing what I'd heard. I'd thought there were only a handful of born vampires on Earth, but it turned out there could be hundreds. *Hundreds of powerful and wealthy vampires – and they probably drink as much blood as they want.* I shuddered.

My already taut muscles tensed even more. Even if we stopped the queen, there were more out there. Lots more.

April filled Dimi in on the rest of Raif's story while I dwelled on the thought of countless born vampires living all over the world. April rolled her eyes when she got to the part about Bane being an unstoppable vampire assassin.

"Bane is just a vile bully," she said to Dimi. "There's no way he's a vampire."

"Bane didn't smell like one," Dimi replied. "But he could be a born vampire. We smell like humans."

"Is that so it's easier to kill people?" I asked coldly. "They won't smell you coming?" The mention of Bane being a born vampire had set my teeth on edge. The idea that yet another supercharged killer existed in the world made my anger flare.

"I-I've never killed anyone…" Dimi's voice trailed off.

April folded her arms. "Leave him alone, Etty," she said.

I sat down. "It's true, though," I replied, raising my voice. Why couldn't she see the truth? "Born vampires are built to kill people! Dimi and all his kind are built to kill people!"

"Well, so are you," April said. "You're built to kill. You've been training since you were little to kill people."

"I train to kill vampires," I said. "Vampires aren't like normal people. Just look at Bane. He was a horrible person and it turns out he's a vampire."

"Bane isn't a vampire, he's just a bully," April retorted. "He puts worms in people's hair and he's mean to people who are weaker than him." She prodded her finger into my shoulder. "And, at the moment, you remind me of him."

I blinked. "I'm not like Bane." I sounded winded.

"Yes, you are," she replied. "We know that Dimi didn't kidnap Bane. We know he had nothing to do with any of this. But you won't see the truth."

"He's a vampire," I said.

"Yes, but he's not evil."

For the rest of the journey, we sat in awkward silence. April's words played over and over in my mind. *You remind me of him.* Was she right? Was I as bad as Bane?

Dimi gazed solemnly out the window. What if he really was a good vampire?

He's not! a voice yelled in my head (it sounded a lot like Mum). *Be on your guard, Etty.*

Finally, the bus arrived at our stop and I led the way to the cove. The rain had stopped and the sun was setting, bathing everything in an orange light. I breathed in the salty air, and the wind whipped at my face.

The path to Seer's Cove was sandy, with long grass on both sides. From the top of the cliff, I could see the small semi-circle of beach and the sea stretching to the horizon. The orange sun glittered on the water.

April and Dimi waited a few steps behind me as I took in the view. It was such a peaceful place, but there was no peace in my heart. My mum was out there somewhere, trapped on a ship, about to have her blood sucked out of her. I drew in a breath and carried on walking.

Dimi and April stayed a few paces behind, walking together.

April's words still whirled around in my head. How could she think I was anything like Bane? He was a bully.

A small voice in my mind spoke up then. This time it sounded like April. *You could be nicer to Dimi.*

But Dimi wasn't a person. He didn't count!

I'm not like Bane, I thought. *For one thing, I'm about to fight a clan of vampires.*

However, each time I tried to reassure myself, that same small voice would whisper quietly that I might be wrong.

The path sloped down to the beach. As we walked, I searched for a ship, but could see nothing.

When we finally reached the sand, Dimi stopped.

"I-I can hear voices," he said.

He pointed. My legs kicked into action. I ran to the point where the cliffs met the sea. As I got closer, I saw the sea cave. It wasn't part of the beach; the cave was further along the cliff, facing out towards the ocean – a great open mouth in the rock.

There was only one way to get there. We'd have to climb across the rocks at the base of the cliff that led to the cave.

"What are we going to do once we get there?" April asked. "There could be a hundred vampires waiting for us."

Dimi, who was standing in April's shadow as if trying to hide from me, stepped out from behind her, his head down. "V-vampires don't travel in big groups," he said to the sand. "Too much fighting."

Affectionately, April laid a hand on his shoulder. I pretended not to notice the look she sent me.

"There are six of them in the clan," I said, "so that means seven vampires if Bane's one too."

Dimi opened his mouth to reply, but then stopped himself.

"What is it, Dimi?" April asked.

"Th-the queen," he said. "She'll be strong. She'll have powers. What if Etty c-can't stop her?"

My fists clenched. Perhaps he really was worried. But all he'd done was make me sound weak. I stepped onto the nearest rock. "I'll deal with her," I said resolutely, but I wasn't speaking to Dimi. "April, I'm not going to let anything happen to you." I held out my hand for her to take.

April's eyes drifted towards Dimi.

"What about Dimi?" she asked. "Will you keep him safe?"

I hesitated. What could I say? My hand still hung in the space between us, waiting for her to take it, to trust me. How could she be so sure about Dimi but so unsure about me?

Dimi shrank into the background, his eyes downcast.

I thought about telling her the truth – that I'd save the two of us before I'd even think about saving Dimi – but we didn't have time for an argument. "Yes," I lied. "I'll keep him safe."

Instead of warming her, however, my words made her brow furrow. April had always known when I was lying. After a pause, she nodded silently and took my hand. Her grip felt slack, her fingers cold. I helped her onto the craggy rock and then she turned to do the same for Dimi. However, he leapt lithely onto the rock without any assistance.

We walked at a steady pace. April was slower than me, wobbling as she stepped from rock to rock. We avoided the patches of seaweed, which were frighteningly slippery to walk on, but my footing was steady. I was glad of the years of training that had strengthened my muscles. Whenever April slipped, I planted my feet and held her up until she got her balance back.

Each rock we walked across took us further from the beach and closer to the mouth of the cave. The sea was treacherous here. Fearfully, April glanced down at the jagged rocks sticking up out of the water. She grasped my hand tightly. Jaw clenched, I concentrated on every step.

If I fall, I could pull April down with me, I thought. It was a long drop and I didn't want to think about anyone landing on those sharp rocks.

The wind lashed at us, bringing sea spray up with it. Behind us, Dimi huddled into April's coat, his hands in his pockets. The yellow hood protected him from the rain, but he was still shivering. He leapt gracefully from rock to rock, never stumbling. His movements were so perfect, he could have been performing some kind of dance.

April saw where I was looking. "He saved my life," she said.

My toes curled. "I know."

The sunlight had almost faded by the time we reached the cave mouth. Leaning forward, I peered inside.

There it was! The ship. It was a modern liner with thick ropes attaching it to the cave walls. The water was much calmer inside the cave and the ship bobbed gently up and down. It was immaculately white, its paint gleaming in the fading sunlight. Up on deck, there was a high platform, which I couldn't make out properly, and a lower deck lit with blue lanterns. The blue light made the cave look alien and unnatural. I could see the outlines of one or two people moving about on the ship, but none of them came close to the railing.

We should be able to get on without being seen.

"There's a path along the cave wall," I told April and Dimi once they were beside me. "The stone juts out from the wall like a walkway. We can follow it into the cave."

They followed my gaze. "W-we have to walk across that?" Dimi asked.

"It's a long drop," April said.

"You can stay here," I told her. "You can stay here and wait—"

"No. I can do it," she said. She took Dimi's hand and he nodded in agreement.

"Once we've walked along the ledge," I said, "we climb

the rope." I pointed to where one of the ship's ropes was bolted to the wall of the cave. It was just above the jutting path.

April tucked her hair behind her ears and let out a huff of air. "Let's go."

I went first, making sure I leaned against the wall as I walked. The ledge was slippery and it was barely wide enough to walk on. One misstep, and I would tumble into the water.

Every noise from behind me had me glancing back to check on April. She was fine, her expression set with grim determination.

I wondered if Dad had realised I was missing yet. What would he do when he got home and realised I wasn't there?

A horrible thought struck me. *If I don't make it back, he'll be alone. He'll have lost Mum – and he'll have lost me too.*

Unable to bear the thought, I focused all my attention on the stone beneath my feet, hoping it was sturdier than it looked.

Eventually, I was within reach of the rope. It was tied to a metal ring that had been bolted into the cliff, and it was thicker than my thigh.

"We'll have to shimmy across," I said.

April caught up with me and squeezed my hand. "What do we do when we get there?"

"We find my mum," I replied.

I was about to grab the rope when Dimi took hold of my wrist. I flinched. His touch was icy.

"Wait," he said. He let go of my arm and took off his sunglasses. In the half-light I could see the real colour of his eyes. I stared in shock. They were purple!

Now I know why he likes that colour so much.

"Etty," he said anxiously, "there's a clan of vampires in there…"

"If you want to stay here," I said, "that's fine with me, but I'm going in whether you come or not. In fact, it might be better if you stay here."

Without warning, he drew back his lips and grew a pair of sharp white fangs.

I stepped back and reached for my stake but he spoke before I could pull it out.

"E-every vampire in there will be super-strong," he said, "and they w-will all have a pair of these." He pointed to his fangs. "Shouldn't we have a plan?"

"He's right," April said. "We can't just go storming in. They could… kill us." There was fear in her eyes.

She nearly died, I reminded myself. *Raif almost killed her. Of course she's afraid! And if we just rush onto the ship, she might not be so lucky this time.*

"You're right," I said to her, "but I don't have a plan."

She glanced out at the ship as if she would find an answer written on its side.

"I-I have an idea," Dimi said. Without his sunglasses, his face was softer, his eyes wide and glassy. Despite this, I could feel myself scowling. How could I trust any plan of his? "Vampires are afraid of witches," he continued, "so if April goes first, she can frighten them."

"I can do that," she said and her eyes widened. She reached underneath her coat and pulled out her grandma's necklace. "And I have this. They'll believe me."

"No," I said. "I don't like it. It puts you in too much danger."

"I'll f-follow right behind her," Dimi said, "and I'll say we came to join the feast. I am a vampire, after all."

"I know what you are," I said coldly.

Dimi flinched. "April and I will d-distract the vampires—"

"While I go find my mum," I finished. It made sense, but the plan was too risky. It meant April would be up there alone on a boat full of vampires. Not to mention, Dimi would be with her. Who knows what he might do?

I turned to tell April we needed another plan. But my heart jumped into my mouth when she set her jaw and then leapt off the path. Her arms scrambled for the rope. Somehow, she clung on to it, and she lifted up her legs so that they hugged the rope.

I'd stopped breathing. "Are you mad?" I said angrily.

"I can do this," she called back to me and then, before I could respond, she started to shimmy along the rope towards the ship.

Dimi gaped at April. "I g-guess I'm next," he said, reaching across me to grab the rope.

"Make sure she's okay," I told him.

Before he could answer, his foot slipped. His arms flailed. He let out a yelp – and fell.

CHAPTER 22

JUST BEFORE DIMI disappeared into the darkness, he managed to catch hold of the ledge. He dangled there, just one hand holding him up. If he let go, he would plummet into the water below.

"Etty!" he called desperately as his fingers slipped, millimetre by millimetre, off the edge.

I glanced from him to April, who was now halfway across the rope and too focused on what she was doing to notice what had happened. I reached for the rope. If I followed her now, April would be in less danger…

I stared down at Dimi.

His violet eyes glistened. "Etty?"

He's a vampire, I thought. *What would Mum do?*

She would let him fall.

Another voice in my head yelled urgently that he'd saved April's life.

I felt as if my body was made of stone. I stared at Dimi. I couldn't leave him, but I couldn't help him either.

Fear was etched on his face as his fingers slipped. He

squeezed his eyes shut in concentration, but when they opened again, his features sagged with hopelessness. I realised with a pang of sympathy that he'd tried to turn into a bat.

His words rang in my head. *I can't do it when I'm nervous.*

He clung on desperately with his fingertips.

"Etty," he said. "Please!"

A few more seconds and he would be gone. April would think it had been an accident – and I would have one less vampire to worry about. No vampire hunters would be killed by him. The most powerful vampire in the world would be gone.

Dimi's face cracked with pain as his fingers slipped from the rock.

I moved faster than I thought possible. I reached down and grasped Dimi's arm with both hands, and with one wrench I lifted him back onto the ledge. He landed on his hands and knees, panting. I crouched beside him.

"Now we're even," I said. "You saved April's life and I've saved yours. I don't owe you anything."

Dimi glanced up, his eyes red and blotchy. "You really hate me, don't you?" he said in a choked voice.

"Well, you're a vampire," I replied.

"And you're a hunter," he said, another tear rolling down his cheek. "You hunt my kind and send us to the worst prison in the world." With that, he struggled to his feet and climbed onto the rope. He wrapped his shaking hands around it, then bent his legs so he could push himself along.

He shimmied after April, leaving me alone. The last scraps of sunlight disappeared below the horizon, plunging the world into darkness.

Maybe not all vampires are evil. That's what April had said.

Shoving my hands into my pockets, I felt for my stake. I'd sharpened it myself, whittled the wood until it had a deadly point.

Would I have to kill with it?

There were no prison cars out here from Hunters Corp. How could I capture a vampire like the queen in the middle of a sea cave and stop her escaping? I'd have to kill her. If I did, all this would be over. Mum and I could chain the other vampires and then call for more hunters.

The queen's a born vampire, a voice in my mind whispered. *She's going to kill you. You're going to die on that ship.*

Goosebumps rose on my skin.

I shook the thought away and listened to the waves against the cliffs. *It'll be fine,* another voice said: *just remember your training.*

Up ahead, I saw that April was almost at the ship and Dimi had nearly caught up with her. They were just two dark shadows in the night, and the weird blue lights cast an eerie glow over them as they got closer.

Mum was on that ship somewhere, and we had until midnight to save her. Drawing in a breath, I wrapped my arms and legs around the thick rope and pulled myself along it. The closer I got, the more that strange blue light drained the colour from the world.

Eventually, I reached the ship and hauled myself over the railing and onto the deck.

My heart skipped a beat.

A few paces away stood three vampires.

CHAPTER 23

ALL THREE VAMPIRES had their backs to me. For now, at least…

One of them was speaking in a low voice. I realised he was talking to Dimi and April.

I froze on the spot, not daring to make a noise. After a few moments, I slowly moved a couple of paces until I was tucked in the very corner of the deck, as far as I could get from the blue lights that hung above. I shrank down low against the railing, trying to become invisible.

I hardly let myself breathe as I watched them.

The vampires wore fine suits made from what looked like a black, velvety material. All three were men: one of them tall and gangly, one broad and muscular, and the third one was somewhere in between, and had hair down to his shoulders. The broad one clearly had to have his suit specially made: his arms and legs were so enormous they would burst out of normal clothes.

"Here for the feast?" I heard the long-haired vampire say

to the others in a posh English accent. "How would a witch and a kid vampire know about the feast?"

I couldn't see April and Dimi's faces: they were hidden behind the vampires.

"We'll see what the queen thinks," the tallest vampire said, and he guided them to a set of stairs further along the deck. It was too high for me to see what the stairs led to.

My breath hitched. They were going to see the vampire queen! This wasn't part of the plan!

I was about to rush after them when I heard Dimi say loudly, "Th-there's a rumour that you have a vampire hunter on board."

The tallest vampire turned around. Finally, I saw his face. He had a long, pointed nose and an even pointier chin. "That's right," he said suspiciously, his weaselly voice going high-pitched. He stepped closer and leaned down so he was face to face with Dimi.

"Wow," April said, "it's impressive that you managed to capture a hunter!"

The man stood up straight and brushed at his jacket. "The queen is very powerful."

"She must be," April said. "But how is she keeping such a powerful enemy locked up?"

The man laughed. "Hunters aren't as strong as they pretend! The foolish human is on the level below us, caged like an animal!"

Mum!

The other vampires laughed along with him, then shoved April and Dimi up the steps to the platform above.

My mind raced. What should I do? If I rescued April and Dimi now, I might never be able to save Mum, but if I went to the lower level to find her, I was leaving them to face the queen. Alone.

What would April want me to do? I thought. It didn't take me long to come up with an answer. There was no way April would put my mum at risk. She'd climbed onto the ship without having a proper plan. She'd been willing to put herself in danger.

It took all my willpower to turn my back on her.

Please stay alive until I return! my mind shouted into the darkness. When the vampires were out of sight, I hurried along the deck and quietly descended the steps to the level below.

I tried to keep myself from thinking about what was happening above. *What if the queen doesn't believe them? What if—*

I shook the thoughts away. I had to focus.

Soon my eyes had adjusted to the darkness. Light came from a swimming pool in the centre of the room, which was lit from underneath. It cast pale, rippling shadows across the walls. In a metal cage that hung from the ceiling, over the pool, was my mother, one leg hanging through the bars. My heart leapt and I had to stop myself running to her. Glancing around for any sign of vampires, I crept closer. That's when I saw who was lying beside her, unconscious – Bane Larkin. She was trapped with him! If he really was a vampire, he'd feed on her when he woke up, maybe even kill her!

Without warning, a door opened at the other end of the room.

A vampire dressed in black fur walked in. I pressed myself against the wall, praying he wouldn't see me. The vampire wore a hat with a single white feather, and his polished shoes clicked on the decking.

"Hello, dear," he said. For a moment I thought he was talking to me, but he turned to look at the cage. "It's time to get you ready. The queen doesn't want to wait till midnight after all." He had a faint accent but I couldn't figure out what it was.

He reached forward with his cane. The end of it hovered above the latch at the top of the cage, but he didn't undo it.

"You have a daughter, isn't that right?" he asked. I couldn't see his face but I had a feeling he was smiling.

"Yes," she replied.

"Vampires have an amazing sense of smell," he said. "Did you know that?"

Mum nodded.

He reached forward as if he was going to undo the latch, but again he stopped at the last moment.

"It's strange," he said. "When people are related, they have a very similar scent. Have you ever noticed that?"

"What are you asking these questions for?" Mum spat. "Just let me out of here so I can kill you."

"So confident," the vampire said, "and so strong. But I'm going to break you."

This time it was Mum who laughed. "You could try."

"Do you like my ship, hunter?" he asked. "Is it what you expected?"

"I'm done answering your questions!" Mum snapped.

"Oh, but I wasn't talking to you, my dear," he said menacingly. "I was talking to the other hunter in the room."

His head spun in my direction. His face was truly horrifying. He was so thin, he could have been a skeleton.

My blood turned cold.

"Hello, little hunter," he purred. "I could smell you the moment I walked in."

In a heartbeat, he was at my side. He'd moved so fast it was as if he'd teleported. I reached for the stake in my pocket, but it wasn't there. Panic rushed through me.

"Looking for this?" he asked. In his gloved hand he held the stake. Lazily, he threw it over his shoulder and then grabbed my arm in a vice-like grip and dragged me over to the pool.

Mum crawled to the front of the cage when she saw me. "No!" she yelled.

She shook the cage bars, trying to break free.

"Oh dear," the vampire said, holding my arm so tightly I had to stop myself screaming. "It must be awful to have to watch your daughter get hurt."

He turned to smile wickedly at me. "My name is Skull," he said. "I would ask your name, but you won't be alive much longer so there isn't much point."

He pushed me a few steps away and then turned and bowed.

I clenched my fists, trying to ignore the fact that my whole body was shaking in fear. Thinking of April upstairs with the vampire queen, I forced myself to bow and took the fighting stance Mum had taught me.

I stared at Skull and tried to pretend I wasn't frightened.

This is it, I thought. *I have to win. If I don't, the people I love will die.*

CHAPTER 24

MUM WAS WATCHING closely. I could feel her eyes on me.

I had to win.

Skull was on me before I could react. Pain erupted in my shoulder and the world fell away as I flew sideways. I hit the wall with a thud and slid to the ground. My body sang with pain.

I crawled to my feet. He was there again. I ducked his attack and rolled out of the way. When I stood up, Skull loomed over me yet again. He punched me in the chest. Something inside me cracked and my stomach flipped as I flew backwards. I crashed into the wall, seeming to hang there for a moment before dropping to the floor. I couldn't breathe.

I was vaguely aware of my mum screaming and the bars of the cage rattling.

I dragged myself off the floor, my limbs heavy and aching, but I couldn't keep upright. I stumbled and crashed onto my back. Lying there, I desperately tried to move. Skull walked towards me. He had my stake in his hand.

"Over so quickly," he said. "I'm quite disappointed."

No, I thought. *This can't be it!*

They were all relying on me. I couldn't fail.

Skull smirked as he leaned over me. I could smell his breath – metallic and bloody. "Goodbye," he murmured.

He raised the stake above his head but, before he could strike, a noise on the stairs distracted him.

It was the tall vampire with the pointed chin and nose. He was dragging someone down the stairs by their hair – their golden hair. He had a huge bunch of it in his fist.

April!

She was struggling, trying to fight him off, but she was no match for a vampire. He tugged her viciously down the last few steps and then held her head up for Skull to see. Her eyes were wide with terror.

"I have a fake witch for you," the tall vampire said. "She can't seem to do a scrap of magic."

"Kill her," Skull said.

The tall vampire grew a pair of glistening fangs and lowered his head towards April's neck.

"No!" I screamed. I leapt off the ground, lunged at the tall vampire and crashed into him. He hit the stairs hard and his head lolled to one side. He was unconscious. Panting, I scrambled up and reached for April – but Skull got there first. He shoved me. I hit the wall and doubled over, unable to breathe.

Through tears of pain, I watched him lean towards April. She shuddered under his gaze.

"I know!" Skull announced. "I'll kill this lovely blonde one first and make you watch. Then I'll kill you."

No! my mind screamed. I wanted to yell it. I wanted to stop him. But I couldn't catch my breath, and my limbs wouldn't move.

Skull towered over April like a spectre. She crawled away, whimpering, but he followed her. He whipped her around to face him and then raised the stake in both hands.

Without mercy, he stabbed her in the chest.

Yellow light flashed like a firework. A swirling disc of light sizzled around April's chest. It came from the necklace!

Her eyes flamed.

A bolt of golden energy shot towards Skull. He flew backwards and landed with an enormous splash in the pool. His body bobbed up and down on the surface. He didn't move. He stayed there, floating face-down.

April gasped and clutched her chest.

I blinked several times. Had that really just happened?

Shaking myself, I stumbled over to April. She trembled.

"I guess... I really am a witch," she said breathlessly.

"Are you okay?" I asked, checking her chest for injury.

"I'm fine," she said. "He didn't hurt me. The necklace stopped him somehow."

"Your gran was right – she said it was a protection charm."

Her eyes kept trying to close as if she couldn't stay awake. "You have to help Dimi," she said. "He's in danger. The Lacuna Gem blocks magic. The queen's going to use it..." Her voice trailed off as if it was painful to speak.

"April?" I said again. *Was she hurt? What was wrong with her?*

"I'm fine," she said, "but the necklace sapped... my energy. Help Dimi... queen has the gem... blocks magic..."

Her eyes drifted closed and her head fell to one side. I lowered her gently to the floor, tugged off the unconscious vampire's coat and laid it over her.

Hating to leave April, I hurried to the pool. Above Skull's floating body, Mum pointed through the bars of the cage.

"The cane!" she said.

I picked it up. The silver handle was cold. Standing on tiptoe, I lifted it towards the top of the cage. I used the tip of the cane to slide the latch across. It clicked and the cage door fell open, landing against the side of the pool to create a ramp.

Mum lowered herself down and pulled the unconscious Bane behind her.

His skin was white, his lips blue. He looked half dead.

Mum bent down and placed her hand on his forehead. "He's dying. We need to get him to hospital."

"What did they do to him?" I asked.

"The queen kept him for his blood. They took some every night to feed on."

They took his blood! But vampires can't drink the blood of another vampire. That meant... "He's human," I muttered under my breath.

Bile crawled up my throat at the sight of him. He was leached of all colour, thanks to the blood that had been sucked out of him night after night.

Yet, as I peered closer, I saw there wasn't a mark on his body. His neck wasn't scarred. Then my insides squirmed when I saw the cannulas taped to his wrists. *They must have clipped them to blood bags and drained the blood straight out of his veins. How much did they take?*

Mum shook her head in disgust.

Once she'd checked him over, she straightened up, her expression severe.

"What were you thinking?" she asked. "You could have got yourself killed coming here! And you brought April!"

"I was trying to save you," I replied, tightening my hold on the cane. "I thought you'd be pleased."

"Pleased?" she said. "The only thing I'm pleased about is that the queen didn't get her way."

"What do you mean?"

"When she realised Raif had brought her the wrong boy, I thought she was going to burst a blood vessel."

"Wrong boy?" I asked, a horrible feeling growing in the pit of my stomach. "She didn't want Bane?"

"Of course not!"

"But if she didn't want him, then who did she want?"

"Vladimir Nox," Mum replied. "It turns out he's real."

My blood turned cold. I stared at her in horror.

Seeing the look on my face, she crossed her arms. "What is it?" she asked. "Henrietta, what have you done?"

Dimi, I thought, panic-stricken. *The queen wants Dimi.*

CHAPTER 25

OF COURSE THE vampire queen had never really wanted Bane Larkin! He was just a human boy! Raif had made the same mistake I'd once made: he'd thought Bane Larkin was a vampire. The day he'd taken him, Bane had been wearing the sunglasses he'd stolen from Dimi. The two of them looked so alike, Raif had got it wrong.

When he was talking to me in the graveyard, he wasn't talking about Bane; he was talking about Vladimir.

The queen had needed Dimi all along. She wanted to turn him into her own personal assassin.

And now I've brought him straight to her.

As I told Mum everything that had happened, her expression changed from surprise to shock to outright rage.

"You've given the queen exactly what she wants," she said. "Not only that, but you've been working with a vampire the whole time. You let one pretend to be a student. You let him trick you into coming here!"

"He didn't trick me," I said.

"You're a stupid girl," she muttered. "And you will never be a hunter."

She turned her back on me and lifted Bane over her shoulder. "I'll take this one. You take April. We'll go out the window and swim back to the beach."

She was already marching off.

My fingers tightened around the handle of Skull's cane. Without thinking, I banged it on the ground. "No," I murmured.

She stopped. "What did you say?"

"No," I repeated, louder this time. "Dimi's a vampire, but he isn't evil."

"All vampires are evil!" she retorted.

"That isn't true," I said.

Mum and I spun in the direction of the stairs when we heard another voice.

"Hunters!"

The vampire with the pointy chin stood on the bottom step. Stumbling drunkenly, he moved towards us, one hand pressed to his head, which was bleeding from his collision with the stairs.

I ran towards him before he could reach April. He tried to hit me, but his movements were slow and clumsy. I lashed out with the cane and knocked him to the floor. He blinked a few times and then stared up at me with unfocused eyes.

"Vladimir Nox," he said, laughing hysterically. "All-powerful vampire assassin!" He laughed even harder.

Mum appeared at my shoulder and placed her hand on my arm. "Henrietta, we're leaving."

I shrugged her off and leaned towards him. "What's the queen going to do with him?"

"Make him drink blood," the vampire said.

"Why?" I asked. "What good will that do?"

"He's a *pure-heart*," the vampire replied, speaking the word as if it had a foul taste. "A born vampire who hasn't had any blood. He needs to drink blood and then he'll turn!"

"What will he turn into?" I asked.

"He'll turn cold-hearted," he replied. "He'll lose his emotions and become…" He began to slip out of consciousness.

I shook him roughly. "Become what?" I demanded.

"A killer," he said drunkenly. "A cold-hearted killer." Slowly, the vampire's mouth split into a grin and he sniggered. "An unstoppable killer… in a yellow fluffy coat!"

I had to stop myself from hitting him. Instead, I stood up. It was the same story Dimi had told me. He'd said born vampires could be good, that they didn't have to drink blood. "Is this true?" I asked Mum.

"Of course it's not true," she replied, but she wouldn't meet my eyes.

"Mum!" I said harshly.

She folded her arms across her chest. "Vampires crave blood," she said, "It isn't possible to have a good vampire."

"Tell me the truth," I pressed.

She ran a hand over her face and sighed. "They call them pure-hearts. Vampires who have emotions. Bitten vampires are all cold-hearted, but if a born vampire never drinks blood, it is said that they're pure-hearted…" Her voice trailed off and she shook her head. "But, Etty, they all end up drinking blood eventually, so it hardly matters."

I backed away. Everything had turned upside-down.

"I can't believe you knew about this," I whispered.

Vampires could be pure-hearts. They could be good…

If Dimi really was a pure-heart, he'd been telling the truth the whole time. He had emotions. He really cared about April and me.

And I almost let him fall to his death, I thought, my stomach twisting with guilt.

"We have to save Dimi," I said. "It's my fault he's here."

"He's a vampire!" she yelled.

"He's a pure-heart!"

"Even if that's true," she replied, "he's a vampire and we hunt them; we don't save them. We're leaving this ship and we're destroying everything on it."

"What do you mean?"

"Once we're back on the beach, I'm blowing this whole thing up."

I stepped back as if her words had burned me. All I could do was stare at her. I searched her face for some sign that she hadn't meant what she'd said. Did she really want to kill everyone on this ship? Would she really sacrifice an innocent boy?

Before she could stop me, I headed for the stairs.

"Henrietta, where are you going?" she asked.

"I'm not leaving him here to die," I replied.

"You've already made enough mistakes," she said. "Don't make another one."

"No, Mum," I said, "you're the one who's making mistakes. Everything I did was to try to impress you. I tried to kill Raif in order to find you. I was horrible to Dimi. I treated him like he meant nothing, just because he was a vampire and you've always told me that all vampires are evil."

"Vampires are killers, Henrietta," she said.

"Well, you're a killer too," I replied. "And I don't care if

I'm the worst hunter in the world. I want to do what's right. Dimi would do the same thing for me."

I stormed up the stairs without looking back.

"Henrietta!" she called after me.

My name isn't Henrietta, I thought. *My name's Etty – and I'm going to save my friend.*

CHAPTER 26

AT THE TOP of the stairs, I walked across the deck towards the queen's platform. I stopped at the base of the staircase and squeezed my eyes shut.

I can do this. This is what I've trained for.

I couldn't see the top of the platform but I knew who was waiting up there – the vampire queen. She wanted to turn Dimi's heart cold. She wanted him to drink blood. But she'd soon find out that her plan wouldn't work. Blood couldn't go near Dimi.

Before I took another step, a terrible thought struck me and I faltered.

Why couldn't Dimi touch blood? It wasn't natural – it couldn't be. Vampires were meant to *drink* blood, not repel it. Something odd stopped blood coming near him – something magical…

April's words rang in my mind. *The Lacuna Gem blocks magic.*

My heart pounded.

That's why she wanted the gem, I thought. *Magic keeps*

blood away from Dimi! If he wears the bracelet, the magic won't work and blood will be able to touch him! He'll be able to drink it!

I realised I was still holding Skull's cane. It trembled in my shaking hand and I pressed it against the deck to keep it steady.

As I climbed up to the platform, I held one hand to my chest to keep my breathing calm. I counted twenty steps before I reached the top. The first thing I noticed was how dark it was. I could barely see.

I clenched the cane tightly as I waited for my eyes to adjust. Up here, the lanterns were red and hung from poles around the edge of the circular platform. They gave off a deep crimson glow that made the world seem deadly. It was a dark light, as if everything was covered in blood.

Suddenly, a huge shadow leapt towards me. I jumped to the side at the last second and found my back against the ship's railing. The shadow snorted. It had glowing eyes. Slowly, it stalked into the light. It was the muscular vampire I'd seen earlier. His neck was thick, his arms and legs enormous. His face was square and he had a wide nose with gaping nostrils.

Snarling, he rushed at me again. I was about to be crushed!

His monstrous mouth opened wide. He grabbed at my neck. I had a split second to react. I raised the cane and hit him in the stomach. Then I ducked low and pushed the cane upwards with all my strength. The vampire roared. His feet lifted off the ground and his arms flailed as he tumbled up and over the railing.

He scrabbled for my arm but I pulled back just in time.

Screaming, he plummeted out of sight. There was a thud as he hit the deck below.

I took three deep breaths. My heart hammered.

Focus, I told myself. *You don't have time to relax.*

Getting into a fighting stance, I surveyed the platform. Three vampires were staring at me. The first one I noticed was Dimi, who was looking at me in astonishment. I saw, with horror, that he wore the silver bracelet, the Lacuna Gem glittering darkly in its centre. It was so big, it had been fastened around his upper arm so it wouldn't slip off. The jewel itself was huge and cumbersome.

I came back for you, I wanted to say, but all I could do was nod at him. Nevertheless, a smile curved the corners of his mouth at the sight of me.

I glanced at the other two vampires. One was an elderly woman in a dark shawl, who knelt opposite Dimi, and the other was a handsome man who leaned casually against the railing. His shoulder-length black hair was swept back and I recognised him as one of the three vampires I'd seen earlier.

I searched the platform but I could see no one else. Where was the queen?

The kneeling woman had milky grey eyes and deep wrinkles. She was frail and ancient. Surely she couldn't be the queen?

The male vampire stepped forward. His dark eyes were fixed on the spot where I'd thrown the other vampire over the railing.

His fangs grew and he pulled a knife from his belt. My muscles stiffened in panic. My body ached. I wasn't sure I'd be lucky enough to defeat two vampires in a row.

He took aim. He was going to throw the knife at me! I

got ready to dodge, but then his eyes fixed on the cane in my hand. Immediately, his arm fell limp.

"Skull's cane," he said, his body stiffening. He seemed afraid. "Who are you?" he asked. "Where is Skull?"

I held up the cane, forcing my hand to keep steady. "Skull's downstairs," I replied, "floating in the pool."

The handsome vampire's mouth hung open. "You defeated Skull…" He backed up against the railing as if he wanted to get as far away from me as possible.

"Where's the queen?" I asked.

The man scowled but didn't answer.

Trying to appear more confident than I felt, I stepped towards Dimi. He was kneeling on the floor in the centre of the platform. He had been stripped of his coat, which lay next to him in a fluffy pile. The elderly woman held a goblet of red liquid – blood. She didn't make any move to attack me. In fact, she wasn't even looking at me.

The cup was full. Dimi hadn't drunk any of it!

I held out my hand to Dimi and he tried to reach for me. There was a clanking sound and his arm stopped in mid-air: his wrists were chained to the deck – his ankles too. He lowered his arm and looked at me pleadingly.

"Release him," I commanded the woman.

Finally, those milky eyes fixed on my face. "That is not my choice," she said in a paper-thin voice.

"Then whose choice is it?" I asked impatiently.

There was a flicker of movement above. Lightning flashed in the sky beyond the cave. Thunder rumbled so loudly that I jumped. The red lights flickered and then dimmed until they barely glowed. Another flash of lightning lit the sky, illuminating a small, winged shape flapping towards the ship.

One final flash and the winged shape was gone, replaced by a mysterious figure who now stood on the ship's railing, bare feet balanced on the thin metal bar.

It was the queen, I was sure of it. Who else would be able to turn into a bat? For I was certain it had been a bat flying through the sky a moment ago.

I couldn't see her face. She was gazing out towards the cave mouth and at the ocean glittering beyond it. She wore a long, black cloak with the hood pulled up.

"Hunter," she said in a deep, feminine voice that cut through the night like a gunshot.

I knew it, I thought with a shiver. *It is her.*

In a display of perfect balance, she turned around on the railing. She didn't even wobble. Her face was almost completely covered by the hood; only her mouth and chin were visible.

The handsome vampire fell to his knees and bowed low.

"Go and check on our prisoners, Lance," she commanded him. She did indeed have the accent of a queen – an English queen.

Keeping his head bent, the handsome vampire backed away and disappeared down the steps.

Mum! I thought, panicked. *Are you still down there?*

"Hunter," the queen said, pulling me from my thoughts, "you were born to destroy vampires, yet you have come to save one."

"He's my friend," I replied, my voice shaky.

The queen floated down from the railing. The platform darkened as if a shadow had passed over it. The red lights flickered.

"What would your mother say?" the queen asked. "I'm sure she would tell you to leave him behind."

"Yes, but I know that Dimi isn't evil."

The queen bared her teeth. "So, am I evil?"

"You... you had two innocent women killed," I replied. "You kidnapped a child. You've been drinking his blood."

"So you do think I'm evil," she said. "You think I'm bloodthirsty."

She swept across the platform in a blur of black fabric and crouched next to Dimi.

"Is it my fangs that make me evil?" she asked, pulling back Dimi's top lip. Before my eyes, he grew a pair of long, sharp fangs.

"He has them too," she said. "They're just as sharp as mine, and just as deadly."

"He wouldn't hurt anyone."

She took hold of Dimi's finger. There was a crack. A gasp escaped my lips. She'd broken his finger! He screamed in pain and his eyes glowed bright purple. He tugged against the chains, which groaned, and his expression became feral. For a moment, I thought the chains would break, but then his eyes returned to normal and he dropped his arms.

He breathed heavily, his body bent forward so he could cradle his injured finger.

The queen became a blur again and, in an instant, she stood in front of me.

"You think he isn't dangerous?" she asked. "He is stronger and faster than you can imagine, and he can lose control."

I wanted to go over to Dimi, but I was too afraid to move.

"You seem to know so much, hunter," she said. "So, tell me. What is it that makes him so good and me so evil?"

Why was she asking me that? Did she want me to tell her it was okay to kidnap people, to *murder* people? It disturbed me that I couldn't see her face, just her mouth, which twisted into a smirk as she waited for an answer. I wanted to see her eyes. Were they boring into me? Could she even see me through the shadow of the hood?

She stroked the top of Dimi's head as though he was her pet. "We're both vampires after all," she said. "Aren't we both evil?"

I thought about Dimi, looking back on the last few days. Everything seemed different now that I knew he was pure-hearted. It turned out he'd just been a boy who'd never gone to school before, who'd lived with his elderly tutor and didn't know that ballet dancing and having a purple lunchbox would make people tease him. I remembered the story he'd told April about his mum's blood running through his veins. He'd just wanted to make her feel better. Then, an image of him saving her life in the graveyard swam in my mind. I saw him holding the tree branch in astonishment while Raif lay on the ground, unconscious.

"It's his actions," I said at last. "It's the things he does. That's what makes him good. Unlike you, he helps people."

The queen laughed. It wasn't a happy sound. It was bitter and full of malice. Once her laughter had died away, the ship fell into a deadly silence. The only noise was the distant crashing of waves on rocks.

"I'm going to tell you a story," she said, "and at the end, I want you to tell me who the real evil is. Unless you'd prefer me to kill you here and now."

My heart skipped. I had a sudden instinct to run, for I had no doubt that she could kill me. She radiated the same sort of power as Skull, except I had a feeling she was even stronger than he was. I'd be no match for her. It dawned on me, in that moment, that I was going to die.

I'd failed. Dimi would be forced to drink blood and become the world's most cruel and powerful vampire, and I'd be dead.

"You're going to kill me," I murmured.

"Yes," she replied, "but not yet. You should die knowing the truth." A humourless smile curved her lips. "So I'll ask you again. Will you listen to my story?"

If I agreed, it might give me time to find a way out of this. There had to be a way to free Dimi and get off this ship. Could I hope that Mum would come to my rescue? No, I couldn't rely on anyone else to save me.

I'd hear the queen's story and come up with a plan.

"Y-yes," I croaked, "tell me."

The queen approached the railing and faced the ocean. "It started with a vampire princess called Lilly," she said. "Her mother was the English vampire queen and her father was a vampire prince from Iceland. The family owned many mansions and castles in England. None of them drank blood. They didn't even eat red meat in case any of the animal blood touched their lips.

"When Lilly had lived for hundreds of years, her parents had another child. Children are rare in vampire families, and so it was a big celebration. After that, Lilly took care of her little sister and watched her grow up. Lilly decided she wanted her own children and so she married a vampire prince from overseas. He came to live in England with her and for over a hundred years, they lived happily. That's when the rumours of the hunters started. People said hunters were stronger and faster than humans and they had weapons that could stun, weaken and even kill a vampire.

"In other countries, born vampires wanted more protection from the hunters, so they broke the old laws and began to create 'the bitten'. They would bite humans and wait for them to change into vampires and then keep them as bodyguards.

"In England, Lilly's family didn't think the hunters were a threat, so they carried on as normal. After a time, Lilly became pregnant and had a child."

The queen paused. I held my breath as she turned and took a predatory step towards me. Her mouth was a thin line. For some reason, I was afraid to hear the rest of her story. I knew it had something to do with me – something dark.

"Lilly's child was barely a year old when the hunters came," the queen said. "They stormed the castle and killed everyone in it. Near the end, Lilly, her husband and her baby were the only ones left alive. The hunters were coming for them and they were trapped, certain to die. And so Lilly did something she never thought she'd do. She drained the blood from the first hunter who came for them, and sucked all the life out of him. She'd never had blood before, but she knew that a born vampire who feeds on it is far stronger and faster than those who don't, and so, with her new strength, she killed more and more hunters, and drained more and more blood until she was completely cold-hearted. There wasn't a scrap of emotion left in her.

"After the carnage, she went back to find her husband. But when he saw her, he was horrified – and she realised that she didn't care. She didn't care about him or her child any more. Her heart had turned to ice. So she fled. She'd saved her child but she'd cursed herself – forever."

As her story ended, my mind raced. It couldn't be true. Hunters would never have attacked an innocent family like that. If they'd known the vampires were pure-hearted, they wouldn't have hurt them.

The queen took another step closer to me. I felt horribly aware of the pulse in my neck. Could she hear it? Did she want to sink her fangs into me?

"Hunter, I'm waiting," she said. "Tell me. Who is the real evil in the story?"

"It can't be true," I said.

"Oh, but it is," she snarled.

"Hunters would never do that, not unless they thought Lilly's family was dangerous."

"Something made them attack that night. Do you know what it was?"

I shook my head.

The queen's lip curled. "A hunter who hated vampires told the other hunters a lie. She said that Lilly's family had killed three innocent men. It turned out the men had been killed by someone else – but by then it was too late."

"Why would anyone do that?" I asked.

"Aren't you going to ask me who the hunter was?" the queen remarked. "Are you afraid to hear it?"

I had a horrible feeling I didn't want to know the answer.

The queen took another step forward. "The evil, lying hunter," she said, pronouncing each word as though it was a curse, "was called Felicity. Felicity Steele."

I clutched my chest. "No."

"Yes, my dear," the queen hissed, "it was your mother.

She was the reason the hunters came after Lilly's family. *She* was the reason they died."

The truth struck me.

"Lilly was a princess," I said. "So if her parents died, she would have become…"

"… the queen," the hooded woman finished.

"You," I said, my voice tight.

"Yes," she replied. "I'm Lilly. I'm the one who lost her family because of your mother's lies." She stepped closer to me. "Oh, but not all my family perished. You've met my father, I believe. In fact, you are holding his cane."

CHAPTER 27

THE QUEEN SNATCHED the cane from my hand. "This doesn't belong to you," she said. "You're a hunter *and* a thief." She broke the cane in half, threw one half to the floor and held up the other. The wood was sharp and jagged where she'd broken it.

Before I knew what was happening, she had me in a firm grip and pushed me into a crouch in front of Dimi. The broken cane was in my hand – the sharp wooden end pointed at my friend.

"He won't drink blood," the queen whispered in my ear. "I've spent all this time finding the gem and now he won't drink. So he is of no use to me."

Dimi was still clutching his broken finger. His eyes travelled down to the broken cane and his face blanched.

"You see," the queen whispered, "the witches put their magic on him. Blood can't touch him. So I found the Lacuna Gem, to block their magic. But the prophecy won't come true if he is forced to drink. It has to be his choice."

She wrapped her hand around mine and pushed the

cane towards Dimi's heart. With all my strength I fought, but she was far stronger than me. The cane inched closer and closer to Dimi's chest.

"No," I begged. "Please stop."

The queen pushed harder. "But this is what you were born to do," she whispered. "You can't tell me you haven't thought about it. He's a vampire. I bet part of you wants to kill him."

"No!" I shouted. I tried to escape her, tried to move my arms, tried to move my legs, but she held me as if she was made of stone. I couldn't escape.

In my panic, I felt a gentle touch on my shoulder. It was Dimi.

The cane was less than a centimetre from piercing his skin but he didn't look afraid any more.

"It's okay," he said. "It isn't your fault."

Without warning, the cane stopped moving. The queen gasped. For a moment, I thought she was hurt but then she spun the cane around and pointed it at my chest.

"I have a better idea," she said. She beckoned to the elderly vampire. The old woman shuffled towards us, the goblet of blood in her wrinkled hand. Bowing her head, she held out the golden cup to Dimi.

At first, he didn't take it.

"Here's the new plan," the queen said to him. "Drink the blood or I'll kill your friend."

I gasped.

As the cup was brought closer to him, Dimi's lips trembled.

"Don't do it," I said. "If you drink it, your heart will turn cold."

He took one look at the cane pointing at my chest and then took the goblet from the elderly woman's hands. He closed his eyes.

"I don't want to be evil," he said. "But I don't want you to die."

Dimi opened his mouth. Slowly, he brought the goblet to his lips.

"No!" I shouted.

Out of nowhere, a black shape flapped between us and knocked the goblet out of Dimi's hand. Blood splashed across the deck. The shape landed upside-down on the railing. I stared at it in shock. It was a bat!

It flapped its wings twice – then its wings grew. They morphed into a cloak. When the cloak stopped spinning, it settled around the shoulders of a man. A vampire.

The queen released me and shot to the other side of the platform. The elderly woman crawled away towards the railings, her thin body shaking. The stranger and the queen stared at each other. After a moment of silence, the man laid a hand on Dimi's shoulder.

"Vladimir," he said. "Are you all right?"

Dimi's eyes began to water. "I'm sorry, Dad," he said. "I-I'm okay."

Dad?

I stared up at the man in shock. He met my gaze with a distrustful look. His eyes were a darker purple than Dimi's and his face was much sharper. My insides twisted.

"We'll talk about this when we get home," he said to Dimi, still staring daggers at me. He had an accent. I remembered Dimi had said his dad was from Romania.

"Lilly," he said to the queen.

The way he said it – it was as if he knew her! Dimi and I exchanged a glance. His father knew the queen?

I couldn't see her face, but she seemed unnerved. "I thought you were in Romania," she said.

"No," he replied. "The witches brought me to Brightwood. To protect Dimi from... something like this."

The queen clutched at the railing. Her legs seemed to give way beneath her.

Dimi's father stepped forward.

"Stay back!" she yelled. The lights smashed, one by one, until the ship had been plunged into darkness. Shadows crawled around her body. Black fog spiralled up her arms.

"It was you who broke into my house," Dimi's father accused.

"I didn't know it was your house," she answered.

"You tried to kidnap my son," he said.

The queen winced. "I didn't know," she whispered. "Your name, your scent..."

"The witches changed them," he told her flatly, "to keep us hidden."

"I had no idea who he was." She seemed to be talking to herself more than anyone else. The moonlight shone faintly on the hood of her cloak. Underneath it, I could see her lips trembling.

"Lilly," he said again.

Her jaw clenched and she rose to her feet. I couldn't be sure, but I thought she was staring at Dimi. A moment later, she swivelled on the spot. Her cloak twisted around her and she shrank into a ball of shadows that writhed in the air and then transformed into a bat.

"Wait!" Dimi's father yelled, but the queen had already flapped away into the darkness.

Beside me, Dimi's brow furrowed. He contemplated the puddle of blood on the deck, and brushed his lips. Next to the puddle, the golden cup lay on its side. He yanked the bracelet off and threw it onto the deck. Immediately, the puddle of blood began to inch away from him.

"It's over," I whispered. "You didn't drink it. You're okay."

He lifted his hand. His broken finger had healed.

"Yes," he said quietly. "I'm okay, I think."

I was about to tell him I was sorry for everything, but I was distracted when Mum appeared at the top of the steps, carrying her stake. She was dripping wet. She must have swum Bane and April back to the beach by herself. Her eyes widened as she looked from me to Dimi's father to the elderly vampire cowering in the corner and then finally to Dimi.

"You must be Vladimir Nox," she said, her tone cold. "You and every other vampire on this ship are under arrest."

CHAPTER 28

MUM RAISED HER weapon threateningly. The stake was made of ebony – I could tell by its dark, almost black colour – and it had been whittled to a horribly sharp point.

"You've been working with the queen," she said to Dimi. "You are dangerous. Your actions have brought harm to my daughter. You will be taken to Traxis. I've already contacted headquarters. A team of hunters is on its way to capture you."

Dimi tugged fearfully at his chains. They rattled but they did not break. I reached for the cuffs around his wrists and tried to prise them open. They wouldn't budge. His eyes were frantic.

"You're trapped here," Mum said. "You will not leave."

"You're a vampire-hating fool," Dimi's father told her, "and one day you will regret the things you have done." His jaw was tight and I got the feeling he was restraining himself.

"I'm no fool," she replied. "And I look forward to seeing your face when you walk through those gates into Traxis. Believe me, you won't be so confident then."

"I will never go there – and neither will my son."

"Oh yes, he will," she said. "And I don't think he'll last a day."

The thought of Dimi in a prison full of evil vampires made me shiver. He wouldn't survive. He was too good, too sweet and kind. How could Mum not see that?

Before I knew what I was doing, I was on my feet. Mum stepped forward but I blocked her path.

"You can't do this," I said. "I won't let you."

Behind me, there was a clank. Mum tried to pass me but I stood in her way.

"Henrietta!" she shouted. She tried to push me aside but I wouldn't move. I grabbed her arms.

"You can't do this."

But she didn't answer. Her attention was focused on something else. I turned to see Dimi standing next to his father. His chains were broken. He scrunched his face up in concentration and then his hair twisted and his shirt turned black. His body folded in on itself. At first, I gasped, afraid something was wrong, but a moment later, he'd transformed into a bat with purple ears and big round eyes. Beside him, his father had also changed.

They didn't waste a moment. As soon as they were airborne, they flapped away into the darkness – Dimi, smaller and clumsier than his father.

Angrily, Mum shoved me aside. She ran to catch up with them but she reached the railing too late. She hung over the edge, staring after the two bats.

"I'm sorry, Mum," I said.

She said nothing. She didn't even look at me.

She lifted the ebony stake and threw it with perfect aim at the elderly vampire. The woman shrieked as it hit her in the chest. Her skin turned grey, then black, and finally she disintegrated to dust. The wind carried the specks away across the ocean. Without thinking, I ran over to the spot and tried to grab the dust, but it blew away on the wind. She was gone. I clutched my throat, my stomach turning over. I thought I was going to be sick.

I'd never seen anyone die before. And Mum had killed her.

I stepped back. Where the vampire had been a few moments ago, there were now only a few flecks of ash.

Mum's shoulders sagged for a moment but then she straightened them and marched off the platform. I watched her leave, feeling like I didn't know her at all.

I breathed in the sea air.

"I'm sorry," I whispered to the last few specks of dust. I brushed them with my hand and they floated off on the wind.

Glittering in the blood-red light, the Lacuna Gem caught my eye, its black surface darker than the night. I snatched it up and hid it in the pocket of my hoodie.

Then I picked up the ebony stake and flung it into the ocean. It landed with a splash and sank beneath the waves.

CHAPTER 29

WHEN THE HUNTERS arrived in their white military-style uniforms, I was taken by boat back to the cove. April was waiting, her hair and clothes dripping.

As soon as I was on solid ground, I collapsed. I lay flat on the sand and drew in deep breaths. I'd never ached so much in my life. My back was sore. My arms were shaky. I wobbled when April leaned over and helped lift me up. Before she could say anything, I hugged her. When she drew away, her eyes were frantic. "What happened to Dimi?" she asked.

A smile tugged at my mouth. "It's okay. He got away."

She raised her eyebrows. "You're not angry?"

"I was wrong," I said. "Dimi's good. He was always good."

The words warmed her features. Her hair seemed to glow with golden light. I gazed down at the yellow crystal hanging from her neck. That's when I noticed the thin, zigzagging crack running through the middle of it.

"Skull broke it," I said.

She nodded. "He must have done it when he stabbed me."

The memory of it made me wince. "I thought he was going to kill you," I said.

"The necklace protected me," she said. "I'm okay."

An image of the yellow light popped into my mind. I remembered the way it had smashed into Skull and thrown him in the pool.

"I'm sorry," I told her. "I was useless. Skull would've killed both of us if it hadn't been for you."

"I'm fine," she said, but there was something sad in her eyes.

"What is it?"

"It's nothing." She tugged at the necklace as if she wanted to pull it off. "It's Bane we should be worrying about," she said. "As soon as the hunters got here, they rushed him to hospital. He looked so pale…"

"He'll be okay," I said, trying to reassure her.

"I hope so," she replied. "I tried to call an ambulance but your mum took my phone to contact the hunters instead. She left me here to wait for them. I didn't know what to do. I thought… I thought Bane was going to die."

"He didn't," I reassured her. "He won't."

We fell silent. A shadow loomed above us – a hunter. He motioned for me to follow him. I didn't want to leave April behind, but I could see Mum in the distance and I didn't dare make her wait. Another hunter approached and said he would stay with April until her grandma arrived to pick her up. I hugged April goodbye and made my way across the beach, where some cars with blacked-out windows waited.

Mum sat in the back seat with me while a pair of hunters silently drove us home. She bunched her fists, her knuckles white. Anger radiated off her in waves. Dimi and his father had escaped – not to mention the queen. Mum's mission had been a failure. As we sat side by side, I wondered if the queen's story was true. Had my mother really lied to Hunters Corp? Had she really pretended the queen's family had murdered people just so the hunters would attack them?

I was about to take her hand but thought better of it. "Dad's probably worried sick," I said.

No answer. She kept her head turned towards the window.

"He'll be glad to see you," I told her. "He even thought about ringing the police when you went missing."

Her fingers twitched but other than that she didn't react.

My heart sinking, I gazed out of the window. It was a still night. The sky was clear and I counted the stars, thinking about everything that had happened.

April was a witch. Bane definitely wasn't a vampire. And Dimi was a bloodsucking monster with a pure heart… so he wasn't really a monster at all. I wasn't sure about his father. There was also the queen. She'd got away. Where would she go? Would she come back? And how did Dimi's father know her?

I thought about her story. She'd had a husband and a child…

A suspicion nagged at me. How old was her child now?

Just as the question entered my mind, I saw two shapes flapping across the sky, silhouetted against the moon – a large bat and a smaller one.

Dimi, what happened to your mum? I thought. *You said she was dead, but what if you were wrong? What if she isn't dead at all?*

I watched the two bats disappear, and wondered if Dimi

had suspicions too. Did he wonder how his father knew the queen?

Had they simply been friends, or had they been something more?

If she'd been his partner, his wife even, then that meant Dimi was…

I couldn't let myself finish that thought. The prophecy said he would become cruel and powerful. Surely, he wouldn't end up having an evil vampire queen as a mother too?

I didn't know if my guess was right. But I knew, one way or another, I had to keep Dimi safe. It didn't matter who his parents were. Dimi was a vampire who couldn't touch blood. He was good and he was my friend. And I wouldn't let anyone hurt him.

As we pulled up outside our house, a voice came out of the car's radio.

"All vampires have been captured and are being sent to Traxis," the voice said.

Mum reached across and grabbed the radio. "Confirm how many vampires in total."

"Three."

Mum thought for a moment then frowned. I tried to remember how many vampires had been left on the ship. The queen had escaped and the elderly vampire had… died. That left Skull, the pointy-chinned vampire, the handsome one, and the muscly one I threw over the railing…

There should have been four!

"The vampire in the pool," Mum said. "Tell me you captured the vampire floating in the pool!"

There was a long silence before the man on the other end

of the radio answered, "There was no vampire in the pool, ma'am. It was empty."

My breath hitched.

It couldn't be possible.

Skull was out there somewhere, alive.

A MESSAGE FROM GRAYSON:

I hope you enjoyed reading about Etty Steele as much as I enjoyed writing about her.

You can visit graysongrave.com for news and updates on my books.

ACKNOWLEDGEMENTS

Thank you to everyone who read and re-read this book in the editing process. Thanks go to my mum, dad, my sister and my nan. Of course, massive appreciation goes to my editor Jane Hammett, who helped me question, reflect on, and flesh-out each draft. Finally, thank you to Mallory Class for being my guinea pigs!

ABOUT THE AUTHOR

Grayson Grave definitely does not live in a cave hanging upside down with bats. He is, in fact, a primary school teacher. Never has Grayson been a vampire. The reason he stays in his house writing books is not because he's afraid of sharp wooden objects.

CPSIA information can be obtained
at www.ICGtesting.com
Printed in the USA
FSHW021731190819
61203FS